Christine McCall

A novel

Helen Hendricks Friess

iUniverse LLC
Bloomington

CHRISTINE MCCALL
A NOVEL

iUniverse books may be ordered through booksellers or by contacting:

iUniverse
1663 Liberty Drive
Bloomington, IN 47403
www.iuniverse.com
1-800-Authors (1-800-288-4677)

Because of the dynamic nature of the Internet, any web addresses or links contained in this book may have changed since publication and may no longer be valid. The views expressed in this work are solely those of the author and do not necessarily reflect the views of the publisher, and the publisher hereby disclaims any responsibility for them.

Any people depicted in stock imagery provided by Thinkstock are models, and such images are being used for illustrative purposes only. Certain stock imagery © Thinkstock.

ISBN: 978-1-4917-1569-7 (sc)
ISBN: 978-1-4917-1568-0 (e)

Library of Congress Control Number: 2013921360

Printed in the United States of America.

iUniverse rev. date: 12/5/2013

Chapter 1

Christine knew that she was one of the lucky people in the world. She had met, known, loved, and been loved by George McCall for more than thirty years. Sometimes she still felt shame and embarrassment about many bad choices she made in her early years. But she had changed that life while she was still young and strong enough to find a new way. Because she changed, she met her George, the man she loved in ways she never dreamed possible. She was so blest that he loved her with the same passion that she loved him. He was twenty years older than she but had never married. She had been married twice. They shared a life that she knew so few people get to experience. Now she was sixty years old and left alone.

She felt a bit melancholy as she drove home from church. It was a beautiful spring morning. The sun was shining brightly and the blossoms on the trees were beginning to show their colors. You could feel and even smell spring in the air. She wished that George was beside her to share this glorious day. George had died exactly five years ago today. That day had been cold and rainy. His last words of love sustained her and gave her the strength to go on without him. Even though he was not physically with her, she knew his spirit and love helped her through each day. She'd feel much better once she got out to the rock to talk to him.

The rock was a crag on a cliff that overlooked the Pacific Ocean. Quite often she and George liked to drive the twenty or so miles from their home in northern California to hike along the coastline to this special place. They climbed up the path on the cliff, and then sat, relaxed, and watched the waves of the ocean come ashore. Sometimes on a bad weather day the waves came rushing in and out, crashing into the rocks along the shoreline, but on a day like today she knew the waves would come ashore very gently and then roll back out to the deeper water. Christine and George loved their special place. They made up stories about the ships they saw on the horizon. Maybe they were cargo ships bringing some exotic wares to the states; or they might be cruise ships filled with happy people. She and George sat for hours enjoying the view. Now she was comforted by going to this special place. She was anxious to get started on her way.

When she arrived home she hustled inside to change from George's favorite outfit: a black pencil-skirt, white shirt and very high heeled shoes. He told her she looked absolutely beautiful in it and wanted her to wear it often. She smiled to herself. George liked any short skirt she wore that showed off her legs. He was definitely a leg man. She caught a glimpse of herself in the mirror. Her hair was still the bright red of her youth. She had inherited good smooth clear skin from her mother. Not a wrinkle had appeared yet. A passing thought reminded her of the times she tried to change the color of her hair to black or blonde. That brought to mind unhappy times, so she pushed the thoughts away. Today was a day to think about and talk to George. She put on a pair of jeans and George's favorite sweatshirt with U.S. Navy printed on it. It was one he had worn many times when they made this trip. She picked up her backpack. She put in a bottle of water, fruit, and a sandwich, along with a couple of books for Joey. Joey's dad ran a concession stand in the parking lot at the start of the trail. Now she was ready to be on her way.

"Hi Christine," Joey called to her when she got out of the car to begin her hike. "Dad said he thought you'd be here today. Can I carry your backpack to the trail for you?"

"That's very nice of you to offer. Thank you. There's a package inside the bag for you so be sure to take it out."

"Hey, Dad, Christine brought me a present," he called as his father came to greet her.

"I thought maybe you'd be here today," Joey's dad said.

"I felt the need to come," she quietly told him. "George and I spent many happy hours on the rock enjoying the view."

"George was a very special man. I can't believe it's been five years he has been gone," he told her, and then turning, he reminded his son, "Be sure to thank Christine."

"Thank you, Christine. Here's your backpack," he said as he handed it to her and then hurried away to look at his new books.

The path to the rock wound up and down the side of the cliff, gradually making its way higher and higher.

Christine stopped to look at a pool of water where six otters were splashing. George had given each otter a name and was able to identify each one from the markings on them. She stood watching them for a few minutes then made her way up the path.

When she met George, she was working as a hostess/customer service manager at a very exclusive and expensive French restaurant in Reno, Nevada. Reno was new to her at the time. Just a few months earlier her boss had asked her to move from Vegas, where she was working, to Reno to help open his new French restaurant in that city. At that time she was just twenty-one years old, alone in life, recovering from a long hospital stay. She had mountains of medical bills. She was very determined to make a new start to her life. She saw the move to Reno as an opportunity to help her put her past behind her. She accepted the offer. Shortly after the move she met her George. She remembered the day well. She had arrived early at work that day and found her boss and his wife talking with a man. They introduced her to George.

"Be sure he gets whatever he wants for he is our best friend," she was told.

There were no bells ringing or prickles running up and down her spine. But over time as he stopped by the restaurant periodically while on business trips, they did become friends. Christine had no plans or even time for a man in her life. Although she was only twenty-one she had been married twice. Both had ended very badly. She set goals for herself. First she needed to pay off every cent of a huge hospital and physical therapy bill. Then she would buy a little white house with a picket fence. Her other goal was to buy a grave marker for her baby girl who died at birth. She would never have a man in her life again. She would never trust any man nor let herself be used by any man. George was a friend of her boss. She would be nice to him. Period. She did change her mind. It took well over a year but she learned what a very, very special person George was.

As she sat on the rock she remembered how their love had blossomed; how he had loved her in spite of her checkered past; how he had showed her the world and always surrounded her with love. She felt safe when he was by her side.

Christine sat on the rock for more than an hour. In a soft voice she told George how she spent her days, about what books she was reading, about church that morning, and updated him about what she planned to cook for two of his best friends. Before he died George had asked Christine to take care of these two special men. They lived in a retirement community. Once a week she prepared a meal to take to them. When she delivered the food it was a time for each of them to share with her some special memory of George's childhood.

Christine sat on the rock that beautiful Sunday afternoon, observing other hikers who were passing by. Some smiled, one or two gave a wave of their hand, and others trudged by not even aware that she was sitting there. *Everyone is busy in his or her own world,* she thought. She lingered for a few more minutes and then made her way to her car to go home.

Chapter 2

Christine felt rather listless the next few mornings, remembering how busy each day had been when George was alive. She remembered how they started each day by reading various newspapers from around the country while having their first cup of coffee. After college he served in the Navy for over seventeen years. Then he was medically discharged. Some years earlier he had become interested in real estate investments. He developed a special talent and seemed to know what property to buy when the price was right. He sold the property when the area was expanding with commercial opportunities. She missed George so much.

But this morning everything seemed different. She seemed to hear George telling her she had mourned for too long. After all those years of traveling around the world, she rarely left the house any more. Well, she was usually faithful to attend church (it was her big outing of the week) but she had done nothing to help in the community or even have fun. She didn't even try to make a new life.

True to her promise to George to look after his friends, Ed and Henry, she made lasagna, fixed a salad, wrapped some garlic bread in foil, and sliced some angel food cake. She prepared three baskets of food. In addition to Ed and Henry, a man named Ron had moved into the same housing complex. He was a man about the same age as Christine who had retired early and moved to the village. He went to church with the men so Christine included him when she delivered the food.

She stopped at Henry's door first. Ed was visiting him so she stopped in to chat for a while. As usual, the talk was about George.

"No wonder George loved you. This food smells wonderful," Henry said.

"I bet you went out to the rock yesterday," Ed commented.

"Yes, I did."

"You know, you changed George's life," Henry said. "He always told us he'd never get married. We knew he was in love with you from the first time he met you."

"That was before he even knew it," Ed added. "George told us he felt weak all over when he saw you. He got the shakes. He said you were the most beautiful woman in the world and it was hard for him to remember that he was twice your age. We worried that he might never marry anyone. He had no good example at home of what a real marriage was about. I'm glad you came into his life."

"You must have been worried that I wasn't good enough for him," Christine said softly. "I did make many mistakes in how I lived my life."

"That never entered our minds. We hoped you would be strong enough to take the abuse I know you got from his mother," Ed said.

"I'm sure his mother had a hard life, trying to raise a son with a husband who was in and out of hospitals so often."

"She didn't raise her son. He was left on his own even as young as four or five. He'd show up at Ed's, Will's or my house early in the morning, and our mothers let him stay all day. He was just six years old when his mother sent him to a military school in the winter and camp in the summer. He only came back home occasionally after that," Henry said. "But it never interfered with our friendship. The four of us were like brothers when he was here. Now George and Will are both gone."

"Our mothers never complained about George being around. We missed him when he went away to boarding school but when he came back it was like he had never been away. He was a very close friend," Ed added quietly.

"He loved you both like brothers. I heard a lot about you and was so afraid to meet you the first time. But you and your wives treated me with more respect than I had ever had."

"We all wanted George to be happy. And you did make him happy." Ed said.

"I remember the first day we met you. We had been begging George to bring you home for months on end." Henry shook his head as he talked. "We couldn't understand why it took so long."

"I remember that trip so well." Christine said. "It was just a few days after we finally realized that we did love each other. I was on cloud nine with happiness on one hand but really scared on the other. I hoped I would measure up to your expectations for George's happiness. I already felt like I knew you. Remember, George and I were good friends for well over a year before we were in love." Christine sat quietly for a moment remembering. "On one hand I felt secure in his love, but I also knew how important you were in his life."

"I remember that day, too," Ed said. "When his secretary called to arrange a lunch for us and our wives with you and George, we all said it was about time. We all were so happy for you both. We knew he loved you and we hoped you loved him."

"I was so nervous that day. I guess I have always lived with the guilt about the many mistakes I made in my life. I never expected to meet someone like him. He accepted me as I was. But I knew you were special to him. I wanted your approval."

"I'm sure that nothing in your past was as bad as you remember it. We knew you had been married before, but when a man waits for forty plus years to get married it's not unusual that a woman may have been married," Henry said.

"George always told me the story of my past was mine to tell. I did make many, many bad decisions. He said he didn't care if I told the world or kept it to myself. It had to be my choice. I felt so secure in his love. When we moved here to Crofton, my life was a new start for me. I rarely thought about the past. Each day was filled with joy," Christine said quietly.

"We all teased him about being afraid to love someone," Henry added. "But we knew how much he loved you by the way he talked about you. I remember one time he told us something about you being sick. He loved taking care of you. We just looked at each other and smiled. We knew then for sure he was in love."

"I remember that so well. I had come home from work the night before with a terrible cold that made me sick all over. I didn't go running that morning. George and I usually met on the trail in the park. I called work and told them I'd not be in that day. About half an hour later, George came to my door with some soup from the restaurant where I worked. He was still wearing his running clothes. George had called the restaurant when he didn't see me on the trail. The chef told him I had called in sick. He told George to bring me some magic soup to make me well. I was so sick the night before I hadn't even hung up my clothes or washed my face. George took charge. He ordered me into a hot shower. While I was in the shower, he made up my bed with fresh sheets and fixed the soup on a tray and ordered me back to bed. It had been years and years since anyone had done any kind acts for me. I remember as he left he kissed me on the forehead and said it had been a pleasure to take care of me. I had never met a man who showed such tenderness." She talked slowly and softly as she remembered. "After that we continued to meet on the running path in the morning when he was in town. Then we began to attend concerts in the park."

Ed, Henry and Christine all sat quietly for a moment. Then Christine spoke.

"When I moved to Reno I was in the late stages of recovery from some serious injuries and months of therapy. There was a nice park in Reno with running paths. Each morning I ran for about four or five miles. One day I saw George running in the same park. We had already gotten acquainted when he came to the restaurant. After that we seemed to meet most mornings when he was in town. We began having coffee after our run.

"For more than five years my life had not been good. I ended up near death at a hospital in Vegas. As I recovered I made a vow to myself to change my life. I set goals. Moving to Reno from Vegas helped me get a new start. Things got much better. George became a very good friend to me. He did not know about my past. One day as we had coffee, I was deep in thought. George asked me what was wrong and I told him I had a baby girl who was buried in Vegas. I wanted to place a marker on her grave. I asked him if he knew anything about how to get one. He said he would pick up some brochures for me. The next day he had them. I found a marker I liked and arranged to have it installed. When he came back to Reno a couple of weeks later and we were having coffee, he asked me about going to a concert that evening. I explained that I had to work as I was taking time off the next few days to go to Vegas to see my baby's gravesite. He suggested that since he had his plane at the airport that we fly down and back the next day. I expected to make the trip in my little old Ford Escort with a million or so miles on it. I knew the trip by car would take two or three days. In a gentle way he insisted on taking me back to Vegas where I saw the marker. Then we went to a park across the street where we sat and talked." Christine felt a tear start to fall, but quickly regained her composure. "I told him the story of my past. It included a marriage to a man who was a serious gambler. The first night as I was working as a cocktail waitress in the room of a casino that attracted the big spenders, I brought a drink to Leo. He won big that night and gave me a tip of $1,000 because he said I brought him luck as he gambled. I had already decided to change my life. I was trying to save money to buy a small two-bedroom house with a white picket fence. The tips went into my bank account. After a few months, marriage and a pregnancy followed. When I was eight months pregnant, one night I rebelled against going to the casino. Leo always insisted that I be there to stand behind him. He said I brought him good luck. He lost big bucks that night and came home and beat me badly. I was unconscious for over two weeks. The doctors delivered my baby, a little girl, but she had been so injured in the beating that she died. I set another goal for myself: to buy a marker for her grave."

Christine stopped talking. She looked at George's two good friends. "I'm sorry. I don't know why I'm telling you all this."

"I'm glad you're telling us," Henry said. "George never told us about your past. I don't believe it was important to him. It was never important to us. But it must grieve you now that you have no one to share your life with since George died. We loved him too and miss him. It helps us to share a part of George's life that he didn't talk about to us. I guess we all have secrets that we hope will stay buried. But once those secrets are exposed sometimes it releases us to move on with our lives."

"It does feel good to talk about it. That same day George and I sat in the park after visiting my baby's grave. I told him everything about my past. George told me he loved me and I told him I loved him. And now you know most of the worst. He kissed me for the first time that day, a day I will never ever forget. A week or so later he asked me to come with him to Crofton to meet you."

Ed began to laugh. "And you also got to meet the witch-lady, his mother."

"George told us about how smooth you were when you met her. You pretended you didn't hear her call you a slut. You reached out your hand and introduced yourself saying you were Christine and you knew she must be a special lady because she had such a good son. We all hooted with laughter when he told us about it. We knew you'd be good for George. You were a strong lady to handle his mother," Henry added.

"Well, I was more afraid to meet you and your wives. But you were all so kind," Christine told them as she looked at her watch. "Oh, my, I've stayed much too long. I must be on my way. I'll see you in church."

Christine left the condo unit and dropped off food for Ron Davis at his house and made her way home.

"George, just because I try to stay busy doesn't mean I don't miss you. I'll always miss you. You helped to make me strong enough to exist without you."

Chapter 3

Christine went to bed that night with feelings she couldn't explain. She decided to sleep on George's side of the bed, then changed her mind and rolled to her side. She moved his pillow to her back to lean against while she tried to pretend it was George. Maybe it was talking about her past today that opened up old memories. Or was it a relief? After all these years, did she need to continue to live with the shame from that period of her life all those years ago? Maybe not.

Still she wasn't able to shake the memories from her mind. She thought about George's mother. George had never talked much about his early years, but he was very open and honest when he did tell her his mom was a snob who loved to embellish the stories she told to the point where they were not true. She loved to spread gossip. George had tried to provide for her needs but they spent little time together. He said very little about his father, only that he was in and out of the hospital a lot. He said he never really got to know his dad. After he left the Navy, George spent a lot of his time traveling but when he was home he stayed in the family home with his mother.

The day they had flown together to Vegas to see the grave marker changed both Christine's and George's lives. It was a day of bittersweet feelings; a day of grieving for her baby but also a day for acknowledging the feelings of love for George; feelings that she had been trying to repress in an effort to move on with her life.

When he had offered to fly her to Vegas she knew she must tell him the truth about her past with Leo Martinelli. She wasn't sure she'd be able talk about it. George had seemed to sense her discomfort and said she owed him no explanations. He kept the conversation light and easy. But she cared for George. And she did not want to live with a secret. He deserved to know the truth about her. They rented a car when they got to Vegas.

Near the gates of the cemetery there was a small florist shop. Christine asked George to stop, went inside and purchased a small bouquet of pink roses and white baby breath, tied with white ribbon. It occurred to her that this was the first and probably the last gift she would ever give her child. For a minute or so she stood in the shop, part of her wanting to run away and yet she felt as if she was being pulled to the grave of her baby. She got back in the car and they drove to the burial site. She began to shake all over. George put his arm around her to support her as they walked to the grave. It was a beautiful day, the sun was shining bright. She saw the cemetery was very well maintained, even in this pauper section. She looked down at the new marker.

Sweet Baby
Daughter of Christine

She stood there quietly, asking both God and her daughter for forgiveness about the lifestyle she had chosen that led to this terrible tragedy.

She felt George come up behind her and place his arms around her. He held her gently.

"It's a beautiful marker," he said.

"She deserved better than she got," Christine said as she wiped away the tears that were quietly falling from her eyes.

"I see a bench in the little park across the street," George said. "Would you like to sit there for a little while?"

"Yes," Christine said very quietly. "I have much to tell you."

She waited until they sat in the park.

"You probably noticed that there was no last name on the marker."

"Yes, I noticed that."

"It's Martinelli," she said.

"That's your last name, too," George said. "Forgive me, but is there something I'm missing?"

"Does the name ring a bell in your memory? Gambling? Crime?"

"Martinelli," George said and then suddenly remembered. "Was Leo your husband? I can't believe it?" He shook his head. "You've carried this secret… I can't believe that you are the woman I read about in all the papers. The horrid beating that nearly took your life; the death of your daughter. Oh, Christine, what a burden for you to have carried these past years." He reached for her and held her tightly in his arms.

She told him about that part of her life. "I was married to Leo for more than a year. After the disaster that ended with the death of both Leo and the baby, I was safe in the hospital and rehab center for almost a year. The first few months the press was constantly at the hospital, wanting to know about me and my past, about the baby, where she was buried, etc. I had book and movie offers come my way. I did not want any publicity to follow my daughter. I thought about trying to change my name. I decided not to get a marker until some time had passed. Even so, I don't want some writer in the future to seek and find her grave. It was a hard decision not to give her a name. So I tried to give her privacy."

Christine suddenly felt a calmness come over her as she sat safely held in George's arms. "Have you heard enough? You've been so kind to me."

"Tell me everything, right from the start, unless it's too painful for you."

Christine started to talk. She held nothing back. She told him about her days when she had returned back to Vegas from a trip home to West Virginia where she had hoped to get over a bad separation from her first husband. That was when she learned about the possible death of her parents and brother in a car accident that had apparently happened many, many months earlier. She had not been able to confirm or deny the report. She was now alone in life. Over the next few months, she worked in various restaurants to earn enough money to return to Vegas. As soon as she did return, she divorced her first husband, Roger. She began to work in a sports bar, then a family restaurant, a restaurant on the Strip, and finally in a casino restaurant. She had never seen so many types of liquor. There were different colors of drinks with embellishments that made them beautiful. She decided to try them all. She became a party girl, going with her co-workers after work to the bars. She remembered waking up many mornings, not knowing just where she was or how she got there. On a few occasions she was alone in the room with money lying beside her purse.

One day she woke up and realized that this was not the life she wanted. She thought about what she did want – a home. A two bedroom house, painted white with a white picket fence. She decided to quit her job. Her boss wanted her to stay; regular customers asked for her tables. Finally, he urged her to work in one of the private rooms where only the high stake games were played. Her only responsibility was to make sure a fresh drink was always at the fingertips of the gamblers. Tips were very high most of the time. She thought about her goal – a house. She decided to work there for six months to save for a down-payment.

The first night she stood behind Leo and he immediately struck it rich.

"You brought me luck," he told her. "Don't move from that spot."

She stood there. He won big and gave her a tip of $1,000 and told her to be back the next night. Eventually, she learned his name, Leo Martinelli. She went back night after night, rarely moving from the spot behind him. He seemed to be on a streak of good luck and her little bank account started to grow.

Eventually she and Leo began to have dinner together, often flying somewhere to visit a special place to eat. One day Leo decided they should get married immediately in one of the all-night chapels. Leo bought them each a new Porsche and moved them into a penthouse apartment. He had it re-decorated to her liking. She had full time help to clean and cook. Even the stores sent professional shoppers to the apartment so she didn't need to leave home. He bought her gifts of diamonds, furs and gold jewelry and enough designer clothes to fill many closets.

Christine felt ashamed and embarrassed as she told George about those days, but she wanted no secrets from him. At first it was easy for her to talk with George. But the worst was yet to come.

Leo wanted Christine to become a blonde. She spent many hours at the hair salon each week. One day she rebelled a bit and did not hurry home. She stopped to sit in a park and skip going to the casino with Leo. He came home that night and started to beat her because he had lost badly. Finally she retreated and locked herself in the bathroom. Leo was very careful to hit only her body and not her face or arms or legs so no one could see her injuries. Of course, Leo was very apologetic the next morning and promised it would never happen again. He took Christine to the doctors who treated her injuries from "her fall down the steps."

"Be glad you didn't hurt the baby," she recalled the doctor telling her.

She had not realized she was pregnant.

Leo was thrilled and immediately had a professional decorator come to plan a nursery. But he still wanted her behind him in the casino each night.

Because of the injuries, her pregnancy seemed long and hard. She had constant swelling of her feet. She found it hard to stand for long periods of time. Leo paid no attention to her condition. He insisted she be there each night.

One night she refused to go. Leo lost badly. When he came home he began to beat, kick, and pound on her body. She lost consciousness. When she came to, she was lying in a pool of blood. She was alone. She called for help.

Christine turned to George as she continued her story. "I know what I tell you probably disgust you. You've been so good to me. I'll answer any questions you have. I want you to know if you decide you never want to see me again, I will understand. I am ashamed of the choices I made. I seemed to have no strength to change my life. I can't go back and change things now."

"But you did change it, Christine." George placed his hands on her face and turned it to him. "You are the certainly the strongest woman I ever met. I know you went through much more. Tell me the rest."

"I woke up about two weeks later. My body was covered in bandages from my neck to my knees. My baby was born alive but had died within a few minutes from her injuries. Leo was arrested for the murder of his child."

"Did you ever see him again?"

"No." She paused and then continued. "It seems he was a low-level member of the Mafia. The Feds offered him a lighter sentence if he told them what he knew about the mob. But the Mafia got to him first. He was stabbed to death by a fellow inmate."

George had pulled Christine closer to him as she talked.

"I wish I had been there to help you," he said quietly as he gently stroked her hair with his hand.

"I was totally alone in the world. My injuries were very severe. I was also being hounded by the police, the FBI and the press. I learned Leo had used me to stand behind him to keep other people from seeing his cards, not because I was his lucky charm. I was embarrassed and crushed. I talked to no one. I shuddered every time someone approached me. I faced at least two months in the hospital and maybe years of rehab to regain my life. I was just twenty-one years old with no family and no money. The IRS had confiscated the penthouse and furniture, clothes, jewelry, etc. and his Porsche because he paid no income tax. When I finally got out of the hospital I sold almost everything I owned (a few things were in my name): car, jewelry, clothes, everything, to start paying back my hospital and rehab bills."

George spoke quietly, "To survive what you went through without the help of friends or family is unthinkable. I know of no other woman who could have gone through such things and survived." He paused, and then continued. "Does this explain why you live so frugally in a tiny, tiny apartment and drive such an old car? Are you trying to pay off past debts? I don't know how much Bob is paying you but I believe he pays his staff well. He thinks so highly of you I can't imagine he pays you minimum wage."

"He pays me well. But I was left with all my hospital bills and no real assets. I kept my eye on three goals: pay off the hospital bill, buy a marker for my baby, and buy a small two-bedroom house with a white picket fence. Now I have accomplished two of those goals."

"You are remarkable. You've done so much all on your own. You…" George suddenly stopped talking and moved away from Christine on the bench. He sat there, bent over with his head in his hands.

Christine sat there quietly. *He's trying to find a nice way to say goodbye,* she thought.

He raised his head and looked at her with such anguish Christine wanted to cry.

"Christine, you are the most beautiful and wonderful woman I ever met. You deserve to meet a young man who can take care of you for the rest of your life. I've seen how good you are with children at the restaurant. You will be a loving compassionate mother. I am not worthy to be your friend."

"George, you are a very good man. When you have children you will be a loving and caring father. I have seen how much fun you have with kids at the restaurant. They love you."

When Christine said this George raised his face to look at her. He looked angry.

"Don't say that! Don't ever say that! When I saw you grieving over the grave of your child it made me wonder if I already have children. I have not lived a chaste life. I was the proverbial sailor with a girl in every port over much of the world. I don't even know the names of most of the women I slept with. I'm ashamed of how irresponsible I have been. I wonder how many children I might have fathered. I am not a good man. But I can't change things in my past. I have to live with my guilt. I have made many mistakes in my life." Then he stopped and looked at Christine.

"Why did I finally find someone I truly love at this late date? I do love you, Christine, I will love you forever. You deserve someone so much better than me. You must have a young strong man who can give you lots of babies. You will be a wonderful mother. I'm old enough to be your father. As much as I wish I could be a father, at this point in my life I shouldn't become one. A few years ago I developed the same heart condition that took the life of my father when I was very young. He spent most of his life in and out of hospitals. I didn't know what it was like to have a dad like the other kids. I don't wish that on any child. You have the right to have lots of babies. You will be the best mother in the world."

Christine began to sob. George reached out and took her in his arms.

"Don't cry, Christine. You will find a young, strong, handsome man. You have your life ahead of you."

"I love you, George. And you are still young enough to father a son and watch him grow. But it can't be with me. My injuries left me unable to bear any children. You must find a young woman and start a family."

George pulled back and looked at her.

Christine pulled him over beside her and didn't let go of his hands.

They sat on the bench in that small park until the sun had gone down. She told him about the anguish she felt when she thought of her past and the mistakes she had made. When Christine cried as she told her story, he dried her tears with his handkerchief. When he became angry and stormy as she told more of her story, she gently massaged his forehead and cheeks until the anger passed.

George rose from the bench and pulled Christine into his arms. They kissed long and passionately.

Finally at last, with their arms around each other, they began their journey back to the car. They knew their lives were changing forever.

Christine was stunned into silence as she walked toward the car. *He said he loved me* Christine thought. *And I responded by saying I loved him. Did we really say those words to each other or am I dreaming?* The word love had not been in her vocabulary since she was a small child. The word love had not been used in either of her two marriages. She never expected to hear it in her lifetime. It had surprised her when George said it but it was equally surprising that she also said it. While the words filled her heart with joy, her mind had a fleeting thought that she might be making a rash assumption like so many others she made that led to so many mistakes. She had never allowed herself to think of George as other than a dear, dear friend. She had not allowed herself to think that they might move beyond the friendship stage. Yet she knew in her heart she was being honest. She did love him. Did she dare to hope that her relationship with him would last? Might it lead to something more? *No, no,* she had thought, *I can't think about tomorrow right now. I love him.*

"Christine," he said as he helped her into the car. "I don't know why I chose my moment of frustration to tell you I love you. It was not good timing. I should have chosen some romantic setting. But, Christine, I do love you. I have known I love you for more than a year now. But you are young and beautiful. I know I'm older and with my heart problems I could be gone anytime. I have been trying to keep my mouth shut."

"George," she said, as she reached out and placed her hand on his cheek, "I didn't realize how much I do love you until I said the words. You are the kindest, most honest man I have ever known. You deserve the best woman in the world. Not one like me. But I will always treasure..."

George interrupted her. "Don't say it, Christine, don't say it." He bent down and kissed her lightly on the lips. "Let's lighten the mood. Do you realize that we haven't even had coffee today? Let's find a place to get something to eat."

As Christine got into the bucket seat of the car she remembered the old cars that had bench seats. If this car had a bench seat she'd be able to slide over to sit close to him. From her bucket seat she reached over and placed her hand over his.

It was nearly midnight as they arrived back at the airport for their trip back to Reno. George returned the rental car and they made their way to the area where he had left his plane. He looked up at the sky. "I love flying at night among the stars. It's so quiet and beautiful," he said.

Christine looked out and quietly said, "We live in a beautiful world."

She sat quietly during the takeoff, but old doubts and fears came back to her. She had made up her mind to stay strong and not become vulnerable again. She wanted no part of living the way she had in the past. She had a good job that she loved, she was saving money for her little white house with the picket fence, she had friends, her health was good, and the list went on. If she allowed herself to enter into a relationship with George could she survive his leaving her when he saw her body? Though the inside of her torso had healed years ago, the scars remained. One doctor who had examined her told her she had more stitches than a king-size patchwork quilt. He had recommended that she have extensive plastic surgery to lower some of the ridges that remained. She did not have any money for surgery. She decided to keep her body covered forever. After all, she had decided to never let any man get close to her again. But what was happening now? She began to shake all over.

George looked over at her and reached out his hand to touch her.

"Christine, I've waited all my life to meet someone like you. I want you in my life. I can wait until you're ready to take the next step. I'll be by your side forever unless you tell me to go away."

Chapter 4

Christine remembered the day following the trip to Vegas; the sun had seemed to shine a little brighter. George loved her. Christine went to work with a big smile on her face. She couldn't help herself. She had joy in her heart. Pierre, the chef, saw her as she passed through the kitchen.

"Ah, Chrisine, vous etes dons l'amour," she heard him say. He rushed to her side and gave her a hug. "At last, at last! You are in love."

"Oh, Pierre, you are so right. I am in love. But how can you tell?"

"The love shines from your eyes. We have all been waiting so long for you to realize George loves you. He is a good man. He will take good care of you. I will fix you a special dinner. Will he be here tonight?"

"He'll be back in a few days," Christine told him.

"Bob and Mimi will be here tonight. They will be so happy for you both."

For the first time in her life Christine felt truly happy. She felt as if she had wings on her feet. She looked forward to his return. He called her two or three times a day to make sure she was okay. She bought a new dress to wear when he came back and she bought a pair of very high heeled shoes since George had already let her know she had the best legs in the world. She greeted him with open arms when he arrived back in Reno.

Christine never forgot that first reunion. George had called from the plane to tell her what time he expected to land at the airport. Christine decided to surprise him by meeting him there. When he saw her he began to smile. She saw joy on his face as she ran to meet him. He dropped his bag to the ground as he took her in his arms. She never wanted to let him go again. But the reunion needed to be cut short. He had pressing business back home in California. He asked her to go back with him.

"Is that a good idea?" she asked. "Won't everyone wonder who I am?"

"They all know about you. It's time they met you."

"Even your mother?"

"Especially my mother. My friends are anxious to meet you. They already know how much I love you."

"George! What did you tell them about me?" she asked softly.

"How wonderful you are. When are *you* going to learn what a good person you are? You don't need to live your life ashamed of your past. It is who you are now that is important."

"Oh, George, be serious."

"Okay then. They know you're half my age, that you were married twice, and that you used to work in Vegas.

I don't care if they know every bit about your past. You can tell them nothing or everything. You are a wonderful person. Don't you ever forget that."

Christine knew that if she wanted to be part of his life she had to face the future. She closed her eyes, said a quick prayer and then took his hand.

"With you by my side, I think I can do it."

Christine always remembered how calm she tried to appear when inside she felt she was about to fall apart. But she packed her bag and together they few to Crofton. When she met the airport crew after they landed, the crew was friendly and teased George about waiting so long to bring home a beautiful woman. Her confidence went up a step. They stopped first at his office. His secretary, Estelle, greeted her warmly with a hug. He took care of the problem and checked his mail. Estelle then advised him that she had scheduled lunch for George and Christine along with his three best friends, Will, Ed and Henry, and their wives at a local restaurant. The men had been complimentary and the women were friendly. No remarks were made about the age differences. They had accepted her.

After lunch George took her to meet his mother. Christine learned that about a year earlier George had purchased a condo for his mom in a retirement community so she would be closer to her friends.

George told her he was afraid his mother might insult Christine but she told him she had lots of experience dealing with angry customers and she would be fine. And while his mother never liked Christine much and was very insulting most of the time, Christine, with George by her side, was able to rise above it. After meeting his mother George and Christine had taken his mother and her best friend to dinner. Then Christine and George had returned to the family home.

"I'm going to get ready for bed," she remembered telling him that night.

"The guest room at the top of the stairs is prepared for you," he told her.

Christine knew the time had come. Either she had to face her fears about her body or she had to leave this man. He deserved better than a frightened, cold woman.

She took a long shower, put on a big, soft terry robe that was hanging on the door. She combed her hair, took one last look in the mirror and then went to George's bedroom. She knocked softly on the door and then opened it.

"Is it okay if I come in?" she asked.

He stood looking at her. She had no make-up on, her hair was damp. Little short hairs were curling around her face. "I have never seen anyone so beautiful," he said with a shaking voice. "Does this mean you are…?"

She interrupted him. "Not quite, George. There is something I want you to see."

She unfastened the belt on the robe and dropped it to the floor. "You need to see the real me," she said quietly. She stood naked in front of him, turning slowly so he could see her torso both in front and back.

George had later told Christine that he had nearly cried that night as he saw the welts and scars covering her body. Only then did he fully grasp the terrible beating she had endured.

When she reached for her robe, he stopped her, picked her up and laid her on his bed. As she lay there he quietly touched the scars on her body. At one point he said, "It's a good thing Leo is dead. I could kill him for doing this to you. Is this why you have been afraid to make love?"

"Yes," she answered quietly. She had planned to tell him she was going to walk away from him, but the day had been so nearly perfect it gave her hope for a future with him. But she wanted to give him an out if he found her repulsive. When she tried to talk he touched his fingers to her lips.

"Christine, these scars are badges of courage. Each one represents a separate incident. No one will ever touch you that way again. I love you so much, Christine. Will you let me take care of you for the rest of your life? Will you marry me? I will never let anyone hurt you again."

Christine remembered that night all these years later. She still recalled their love-making. She knew she'd love him forever. They had spooned their bodies together as they slept in his big bed that night and the next and all the nights for the rest of his life. She missed him so much.

Chapter 5

Another Sunday had arrived. Christine put on a dress of sky blue with long sleeves and a slight flair to the skirt. She added a gold chain to her neck and looked in the mirror. Her workouts, required from her injuries of years ago, kept her body young and fit. She looked at her legs. She was lucky, no veins, cellulite, or lumpy skin were showing on her legs. *My life since George has been gone has been one of going through the same routine day after day. This is not good. George and I had such a variety in our lives that we looked forward to each day as something special. I need to make some changes. And I should do it today. No, not should, but will do it. I'll start today.*

Instead of sitting in her usual pew at church she sat in a seat on the opposite side of the sanctuary. She sat next to a couple whom she had certainly spoken to in the past but never had a conversation with, Betty and Ray Coleman. As the postlude ended and they made their way for the coffee hour, Betty spoke to her.

"Christine, Ray has wanted to talk with you for some time. He is on the board of the library/museum. We've heard that George had a very large collection of books, including some old classic first editions. Ray would love to see the collection but has hesitated to ask you about it. May he call you this week to talk about them?" Betty asked.

"Well, of course," Christine answered. "But why don't we just plan now for a time when you both can stop by and see the books?"

"He will be a happy man. Let's tell him."

***

Ron Davis stood in the corner of the room watching Christine as she talked with Betty. This was something new. Christine usually sat on the other side of the sanctuary. And she always made her way directly to the coffee pot where Ed and Henry were waiting (and their daughters were watching to make sure Christine didn't seduce their dads). He had a slight smile on his face.

"Dad, why are you standing there looking so smug? What are you plotting?" His daughter, Marilyn, came up and put her arm through his.

"Me? Plotting? Never," he said with a smile. He kept his eyes on Christine as she talked with Betty and Ray and then moved to the coffee pot. "Have you ever noticed how men respond to Christine?" he asked. "I'm going over to ask her out for lunch."

"Dad, are you sure? Don't you remember what George's mother said about Christine looking for a husband? Come on, it's time we head for home. The kids will all be home today."

"Relax, Marilyn. I need her to help me on a very special job."

"What job?"

He ignored her question. "Look at that. When Christine talks with someone, especially men, they suddenly get a smile and stand taller. She will be perfect for the job I have in mind."

"Dad, you are up to something."

"I certainly hope so," he answered. "I'll talk with you later in the week."

***

Christine stood talking and laughing with Ed and Henry as Ron approached them.

"You look like you're having fun. Is it a story you can share?" Ron asked.

Henry answered, "We were just telling Christine about the time we broke a couple windows at my house. George, Ed, Will and I were playing ball in the front yard where we weren't allowed to play. Will threw a really hard ball and Ed missed catching it and it went zooming into a window. It shattered both the upper and lower frames. My dad was so furious. We weren't laughing that day."

Ed spoke up. "Henry's dad always turned everything into a lesson. He made us learn how to replace broken window panes. At least we didn't have to pay for the glass since he got free labor on getting the replacements."

"I don't think any of us ever forgot how to replace window panes," Henry said with a smile.

"I don't think I heard that story before," Christine said.

"Well, I can't tell it nearly as good as George could tell it," Henry said. "Did you get to know George?" he asked Ron.

"Not very well," Ron answered. "But certainly everyone in town knew of him."

True to routine, the daughters of Ed and Henry came and pulled their fathers away.

Ron turned to Christine. "I want to thank you for the good food you bring to me. You are really a great cook,"

"It's my pleasure. I told George I'd fix something special each week for Ed and Henry. Your condo is in the same area and I usually have extra portions cooked. I'm glad you enjoy it."

"Well, I do enjoy it. Will you let me show you my thanks by having lunch with me today? I thought we might try the new diner down on Sixth Street. Of course, if you're too busy…"

Christine thought of her resolve to get a new routine.

"Thank you. That sounds very nice."

As they ate lunch he asked her about how she spent her days. She told him that her days were pretty quiet since George had died.

Ron spoke. "I volunteer my services at a special nursing home in the area. All of the patients are veterans who have become permanent residents there. The official VA hospital is many miles away in San Francisco. Since these men are not critically ill, the nursing home has been opened for them."

"What do you do there?" she asked.

"Mostly paperwork. I try to make sure that both the veteran and his family are getting the benefits they're entitled to have. If they have home worries I'll try to help if I can. I usually spend each Thursday working there. Most of the men have few if any visitors so I try to stop in to say hello."

"Do they have families in the area?"

"The younger men do but some of the older vets have few visitors."

"It must get lonely for them."

"There are four special men there. They served during the Korean War. They cling together in one unit. One spends some days in bed, but the others get around pretty good."

"They must miss their families," Christine said.

"I try to visit with them when I can," he said. "As a matter of fact I'm planning to go visit them today. Would you like to go meet them? They'd be thrilled to have a female face come to see them. Or do you already have plans for this afternoon?"

Christine sat quietly for a minute or so. She could almost hear George telling her to go. "I'll go," she said quietly.

The nursing home was set in the center of a very large lot with a green lawn. There were some flowering bushes and big trees. The yellow forsythia was in full bloom and some bright tulips bloomed along the pathway. Once inside the building they walked down a long hallway. She saw a large room at the end of the hall that overlooked a wooded area outside of big picture windows. The sun was shining through the trees onto a path that had flowers and bird feeders along the way.

"Brought you company," Ron called out as he entered the room.

"I think I've died and gone to heaven," one called out.

"I'm Mel. What's your name, beautiful lady?"

"I'm Christine," she said reaching out to shake hands with Mel. She introduced herself to Bruce, Chuck and Kenny, who was in a wheelchair.

As she moved from man to man she took time to say something personal to each one.

"It's such a beautiful day. Why aren't you outside enjoying it?" she asked.

"We're not allowed to go outside by ourselves," Bruce told her. "I guess they're afraid we'll run away from home."

"Well, maybe I'll come back this week and take you out," she said.

"Will you bring me a cigar?" Chuck asked.

"How about a piece of pie or cake instead?" she asked.

Bruce spoke up. "I haven't had a piece of lemon pie for years."

"Why not chocolate cake?" Kenny said. "It's good for your soul, you know."

"How about you, Mel? What's your favorite?"

"Who cares about food? I'd like a racing form. It's hard to sit and listen to the races when you don't have information on the horses."

"Well, I don't know about all those requests. But I do know one thing. I'll drive back out here this week and if the weather's good each one of you will get a chance to go outside. Fresh air is good for everybody."

As Ron and Christine left the building to return home, she turned to him and said, "Thank you for bringing me here today. I know I need to do more with my life than sit home and grieve for George. It will give me great pleasure to bring something special for these men. I guess it would not be a good idea to bring Chuck a cigar."

"It would be a terrible mistake. He has serious lung problems. But can you really get a racing form for Mel?"

"George had friends in many different circles. It will not be a problem."

"Mel spends most of his day listening to his radio. He's always trying to find a station that broadcasts the races. It drives the other guys crazy because he usually keeps his radio turned up to a high volume."

Christine went home that night feeling a new energy and enthusiasm.

The next morning that new energy gave way to making her take a fresh look at her surroundings. This house had been her home for thirty years but she had really done very little to change it. Appliances had been updated and computers and a big-screen TV were added. But the furniture remained the same. She had replaced the dark, dreary drapes that covered the windows in the library and the room was a little brighter than it had been. Christine and George lived each day to the fullest. Decorating the house was low on their priorities.

Right after she and George were married they immediately began to travel the world. Once a year they had a major trip; Africa, Australia, the Far East, and Europe. George had served in the Navy for almost eighteen years. Then he was medically discharged because of heart problems. He wanted Christine to share with him the places he had been and the things he had seen. Their favorite place to go was a small country home in the south of France that overlooked the Mediterranean. It was the family home of Mimi, who had married Bob Simpson. Bob owned the French Restaurants in Vegas and Reno where Christine had worked. Bob was George's roommate through military school and four years at the Naval Academy. Bob and Mimi became dear friends to both Christine and George. When they learned that George and Christine were to be married they insisted the two had to spend a month in Mimi's family home on their honeymoon. It was beautiful: a really special place and they went back every couple of years. In between their big trips, George still traveled to small towns and big cities in the United States looking for business opportunities. Christine traveled with him. They were so happy to have each other.

But as Christine stood looking at her house this morning she thought of many ways to make the house brighter and more cheerful. George would be pleased. She looked back on how different this week had started.

She went to the kitchen and started to make some small pastries which she served with tea when Betty and Ray arrived to see George's collection of books. Ray was impressed with the collection of the books on the Civil War. Betty was more interested in the collection of books that were on different countries of the world.

"Did you really visit all these countries?" Betty asked.

"Yes. We usually tried to get the books before we went so we knew which places we wanted to see," Christine told her.

"I'm getting an idea," Betty said. "Did you bring home souvenirs from most places?"

"Yes, we did. They're scattered all over the house. I really don't know what to do with them all now that George is gone."

"Did you hear that, Ray?" Betty asked.

"I heard you, Betty," he answered, "and I bet I know what you're thinking."

Betty just smiled.

Ray said, "I'd better explain things. The mayor has asked me to chair a committee to come up with ideas for an event or two: something the whole town could be involved in helping with. We'd like something a bit meaningful so everyone will be proud of our community. Some of us believe that many people in town don't know about the library/museum and other historic places in town. The committee met recently trying to think of ways we can make the people aware of these gems. We know we need to make it interesting. But a main goal is to get people involved with each other. We want people to know one another as well as the history of the place."

Betty then spoke. "Ray has always been interested in the history of the Civil War. We believe that our town was settled just after the war. He thought about having a series of lectures on the war and then how the town was settled. And if not a series, at least an event with that as the subject."

"I bet we can do a whole series using George's books on the Civil War," Ray said.

"I believe George has an old Civil War uniform and maybe some other items in the attic," Christine told him.

"I bet there are other families in the area with relics from that time period. I know we can attract an audience," Betty said. "Yet I think it might be rather dull."

Christine suddenly got an idea. "It might be quite nice. Why don't you serve some food that is made from recipes from that time era? You might serve snacks or even a sit-down meal. I love to cook. I'll be glad to research and prepare the food."

"You're a genius to think of that," Betty said.

"George and I attended a similar type event many years ago. They had the meal spread out in three sections. Between section one and two, three couples came on stage and sat in rocking chairs. They came back again between the second and third section of the meal. One couple portrayed a couple from the north, one a couple from the south, and the other was a slave couple. The couples did not interact, but simply sat in two rocking chairs and talked first about living near the battle fields. It was all very low-key with no talk of the causalities, but how the war had affected their lives. The second section was their hopes for the future after the war ended. It was really very effective."

"I just knew coming here today was going to be good," Ray said with enthusiasm. "We could do it first and later in the season have a similar to-do with a trip around the world. With the books you have on the different countries along with a souvenir or two from that country, I believe we will attract many people to come to hear about your trips. Will you be able to help us?" Ray asked.

"I'll certainly be happy to lend you the books and souvenirs, but I'm not a public speaker," Christine said.

"Christine, you can charm anyone. You are a delightful person. I know you would attract quite an audience." Betty said.

Christine got really enthused about the new project. After Betty & Ray left, she decided to look through all the books. She knew she had many books to contribute to the library, either for their reference shelves or book sale. Who knows? She might even get interested in redecorating the library in her home to make it lighter and more up to date. She really must try to spruce up the place.

As she ran her fingers over the tops of the books she came upon a small book that was out of place. She pulled it out and began to smile. It was a small book about dieting written by a doctor. She had found it on a sale table one day when she was feeling fat. George had seen it and told her she was not fat and must not have the book. But he started to look at it. He paid a dime for it. When they got home he called for Christine and asked her to bring her tape measure with her. The good doctor who had written the book had included his version of the perfect body size: height, weight, distances between foot and knee and knee and hips, etc. George began to measure Christine's body. She fit every one of the doctor's measurements. They had begun laughing hysterically. From that point on in time, he constantly told Christine she had the perfect body and he had the proof. After all these years it still made Christine smile. *I guess I'll keep this book* she thought.

The next day she called the Veteran's Home and asked to speak to the dietician. She explained she wanted to bring something for Ron's special friends but didn't want to bring something they should not have. She went shopping for the ingredients she needed. She called the friend of George who had connections in the horse racing world. He arranged to get some forms for the races this weekend and gave them to Christine along with a small radio with earphones.

"Give these to Mel with my best wishes. I'll try to mail him racing forms from time to time," he told her.

The next morning she loaded her car with the radio with earphones for Mel, some chocolate cake for Kenny, lemon pie for Bruce and some dietetic cookies for Chuck since he had diabetes and needed a special desert.

As she entered the room they were quite excited to see her.

"Where's my cigar?" Chuck asked.

"I brought you cookies instead. If I brought you a cigar you'd smoke it and smell up this room with stinky smoke and you couldn't smell my new perfume," Christine said as she leaned over him shaking her shoulders back and forth trying to make sure he smelled a small whiff of the scent.

"Oh, that smells good," he told her, apparently realizing he would get no cigar. "These cookies look just like the kind my mother used to make."

She managed to get them all outside at one time. The day was beautiful and the conversation was cheerful. She left them feeling very good about what she had done. That night the phone rang.

"Christine, it's Ron Davis. I just got a call from Ruth King. She's the social director at the nursing home. She's a happy lady. She said she had run out of ideas to try to get those four guys interested in anything but they all were beaming when she saw them late today."

"Thanks for calling, Ron. I'm glad to hear they didn't think I was a pest. They are really such interesting people. Each one has such a different story yet they share such a troubled past. I'm planning to go visit them again next week."

"Is it okay if I give Ruth your phone number? I believe she wants to call to thank you."

"Of course," Christine said, "I'll be happy to talk with her."

As Christine got ready for bed that night she looked back on her week. She had been busy, very busy, and she had loved every minute of her week.

"George, just because I'm busy doesn't mean I don't miss you. I'll always miss you. You helped to make me strong enough to exist without you. But I'd gladly exchange all the nice things that happened this week for just fifteen more minutes with you," Christine said as she looked at his picture.

Chapter 6

Christine was planning menus and making a grocery list when she got a phone call from Ruth King, the social director at the VA home.

"I'm calling to thank you so much for visiting us and bringing so much pleasure to our four special friends. I actually heard them laughing together after your visit. They were discussing your perfume. They have very, very few visitors. You really brightened up their day," Ruth told her.

"It's my pleasure to do it. I hope you don't mind if I keep coming back to see them. And I hope it's OK that I take them outside for a while. It gives me some time to visit with each one individually."

"I think it's wonderful." Ruth paused for a moment. "Actually, I have a motive for calling you today. I've been doing my job for a long time and I'm running out of ideas to keep morale up. I was wondering if you have time for coffee sometime this week so I can pick your brain. Memorial Day will soon be here and I want to do something to make it special. I'd appreciate any ideas you might have."

"I'll be very happy to meet with you. I've never done anything like that and I'm not sure if I'd be of much help," Christine told her.

They planned to meet the next day at a local coffee shop. Ruth was waiting when Christine got there.

"I guess I forgot to tell you something important yesterday," Ruth said. "I operate with practically no budget. We need to go cheap," she continued with a smile.

Christine brought out a small yellow legal pad and said "Well, let's start with a bunch of crazy ideas and see where it goes."

She started to write: Dancing girls.

Balloons

Ruth started to laugh. "That would be a riot. I guess I was thinking along lines of little American flags on plates."

"Too dull," Christine said. "How about a musical program?"

"Do you sing?"

"No, but I know some singers. Maybe we can find a quartet to come and sing patriotic songs. I think I know someone I can ask. Is there a place where they gather in one room or should the singers move through hallways?"

"Usually our programs are held in the dining room but the hallway idea sounds good too. Many patients don't leave their rooms."

"How about having some desserts and coffee in the dining room? Does that make for a problem?"

"It's definitely doable. When will you be able to confirm getting the singers?"

"I'll make some calls this evening."

The women visited a while longer and then Christine had to leave. She had a meeting scheduled to plan the Civil War dinner with Betty and Ray and the board members of the museum.

As she drove to meet with the committee, she realized she was having fun. She liked being so busy. She began to review in her mind the menu ideas she had come up with for the Civil War dinner. There were many questions in her mind. Was it to be a sit-down dinner or a buffet? Was the program to be at the beginning, end or during the meal? What type of budget was set for the food? Christine had already planned menus to cover a variety of plans. She had checked out some food prices. She felt she was prepared with quite a few choices.

Christine was surprised that she knew so many of the board members. Some had been good friends of George. George and Christine had not been social butterflies and she had lost contact with them after George died. It was nice to see them again. They decided to have the gala at the start of the fall season. The committee members were surprised to be offered so many choices not only for the food but for the way it was to be served. They liked the idea of the conversational play. One of the members said she'd write a scenario for it. Another member said he knew some local actors. He'd direct the play. As they left the meeting they decided their party would be the social event of the year. They might even give the guests an option to dress in a Civil War fashion. They began to plan a lot of publicity for the event.

Betty and Ray returned home with Christine. They all were full of enthusiasm and ideas about the upcoming event. Together they went to her attic where Christine found the old Civil War uniform along with a mess kit, a blanket and a few other relics they might use. Betty began to notice other items she found interesting.

"You have quite a treasure trove up here," Betty said.

"I have so many things I don't know what to do with them all," Christine said. "Look at that collection of vases. I'll never remember why we bought vases in so many countries."

"What a beautiful big Cloisonné vase. That must have come from the Far East."

"Yes, it did. I think we got it in China. We bought two of them to set along the fireplace. But I never got around to decorating the room to show them off. Then I broke one and brought the other one up here. Someday I'm going to find a mate for that one and really show them off," Christine said.

"This is a beautiful little chest," Ray commented as he picked it up. "I bet you could get a fortune for some of these things if you ever decide to sell them."

"Maybe I'll just clean them up and use them when the museum has their round the world dinner," Christine said with a smile.

"I do believe you have enough items for a complete show," Ray said with a laugh.

That night Christine then turned her thoughts to the Memorial Day celebration at the VA home. She decided it should be interesting and fun and yet low key. Many of the men and women there had lost family and friends in wars. Most all of them had scars of one form or another. She wanted the celebration to be respectful and tasteful, yet there had to be an element of fun or entertainment.

Christine knew that Henry, George's friend, had a daughter who taught music at the local college. She called Henry to get Laura's phone number and called her.

Laura, who was always suspicious of Christine's attention to Henry, was very surprised to hear from Christine. When Christine asked for her help she became very enthused about helping with the program. She said she would confirm details with Christine by the end of the week. The event turned out to be a wonderful patriotic program with four young men singing and playing the keyboard and/or guitar that they brought with them. They involved the men who lived there in their banter. Before they left they walked into the area of the more seriously ill and did bedside visits. Christine ordered plates of small pastries and punch to be served to the residents. It was a very festive occasion. But nicest of all was when Laura called Christine to ask if she thought the group was OK.

"The program was very successful," Christine told her. "Thank you so much for arranging it."

"Will it be OK if I plan a program for the Fourth of July?" Laura asked.

Christine was happy to tell her it would be a wonderful gesture.

"Christine, may I confess something and apologize to you?"

"Whatever do you mean?"

"Well, I guess shadows of your mean mother-in-law have stayed in the ears of some of us women. She always told us that because of the big age difference between you and George that you'd try to seduce our husbands as soon as George was gone. You are a very beautiful charming woman. I'm afraid we have been very unkind to you. His mother was a mean old woman. Out at the home I could really see how much pleasure and joy you bring to a group of very lonely men. You bring smiles to their faces. I am sorry I misjudged you. Please forgive me."

"Thank you for the compliments, but Laura, don't give it another thought. His mother was just a lonely old woman. I think she probably had a very hard childhood. There will never be another man in my life. The love George and I shared will last me for the rest of my life. He was a very special, good man."

Later that same week Christine thought of how little she knew about the families of her four friends at the home. She had been told they had no family visiting them for years. The next day, after she got all four outside and seated comfortably, she noticed that Chuck and Bruce were engaged in some deep conversation and Mel was listening to the races. She went over to sit by Kenny who was in his wheelchair.

"How long have you been here?" she asked.

"Too long," he answered. "I was in the VA hospital in San Francisco for what seemed like years. The treatments I got were good but the old knee ailments kept popping up and I'd be back in the hospital for another six months or so. My family was not able to visit me often because of the distance. After they opened this home, I was transferred here. And I've never left."

Christine was not sure what to say. She knew nothing about his injuries or home life.

"Tell me about your family," she asked him.

"My wife is gone. We had a son together. He's married now and has a son."

"Does your son come to visit you?"

"I won't let him come. I don't want him burdened by an old man in a wheelchair. I want him to be a good father and spend time with his son. I want him to do things like going fishing or going to a ballgame with his son. Things that I wasn't able to do with him."

"Does he live in the area?" she asked.

"He was transferred to San Francisco. After my wife died he tried to get me to transfer to the VA hospital there. I won't do it," he said stubbornly.

"Why don't you call him just to talk?"

"I will not do that. It's better if he's not bothered with me."

Christine sat quietly thinking.

"Do you think you were a good father?" she asked.

"No, I was a terrible father. I couldn't do anything because I have been in and out of hospitals constantly ever since the Korean war."

"That must have made life very difficult for him. Did he end up in jail or commit any crimes?"

"Of course not. He had a good mother. She was a wonderful woman who made him study. He's a successful man today."

"If you were in and out of hospitals you must have spent some time with him. You must have a few good memories of doing things with him."

Kenny sat quietly for a few minutes. Then quietly he said, "I do. I do have nice memories. He was a good child."

"And I bet he is a good man. Would you like me to call him just to find out if he is OK?"

"No, no. It's better to have no contact."

"Kenny, I don't agree. When we have someone we love we should hold on to that love for as long as we can. Why don't I try to contact him just to see if he has more kids or where he works? We don't have to plan any big family reunion. Just a quick check to make sure everything is OK."

Kenny finally asked the nurse to get his son's phone number for Christine.

With the phone number in her purse Christine made her way home wondering if she really could bring about a reunion of father and son. Her first thought was that she was happy for Kenny. Then she had another thought: *I hope I'm not setting Kenny up for a big disappointment.*

The VA administrator at the home had given Christine both a home and work phone number for Kenny's son. It was evening so she dialed the home number.

"Hello. My name is Christine McCall and I volunteer at the VA Home where Kenny Somers is a patient," she told the woman who answered the phone.

"Oh, dear. Is Dad OK? Is something wrong? Let me get my husband."

"This is Ken Somers. Is my dad with you?"

"No, Ken. Your dad is doing well. I go to visit some of the men. Today I had a long talk with Kenny and he told me about you. I told him I thought I should call you and let you know he is doing well. He appears to be getting very good care. He has three close friends he spends each day with, all of whom fought together in Korea. He finally agreed to let me call you. Do you have any message you'd like me to give him?"

"My dad won't let me come to see him, you know."

"He told me that."

"He is so stubborn. My wife and I drove to Crofton with our baby son and he refused to see us. We drove up from San Francisco many times only to be told he would not see us. I guess the message you can give him is that I want to come to see him. I want him to know my wife and I want him to meet my children and his new great-grandson. I want him to know how much my mother missed him and begged us to bring him home. He hurt us all when he cut us out of his life."

Christine wasn't sure what to say. She remembered the pain she felt when she learned of the death of her birth family. Here is a family that has also suffered a loss. Is it better to leave things alone than for young Ken to come see his father and be rejected? Maybe he has made peace with the situation. He might not be able to take another rejection. Then she thought of Kenny, sitting in a wheelchair all day with no family to ever visit him.

"Ken I don't want to intrude in your life. You have good reason to not come to see your father. Perhaps I made a mistake by calling you. I saw a lonely old man with no family that I knew about. When he talked about you he got a soft look on his face. He is sure you are a very successful man because you had a good mother. I'm sorry if my call is causing you pain."

"I do want to know about him. My only contact has been with the home administrator who cannot tell me about him; who he spends his day with, what he does all day…"

"Ken, let me leave you my phone number. I try to spend a little time with him each week. If you have questions I'll be happy to try to get the answers for you. He was very reluctant to let me call you, yet I think he was also happy when I pushed the issue. Do you have any message you want me to tell him?"

"Do you think he will see me if I come up?"

"I'm not sure. I'll be glad to ask him."

"I don't know what to do, Christine. Let me talk with my wife and call you back."

Christine had a very restless night. *This is what I get for trying to be a busybody,* she thought.

The next morning around 9:30 she was busy with her chores when she heard the doorbell ring. She saw a stranger at the door. He was tall and nicely dressed. She opened the door.

"Christine McCall?" the visitor asked.

"Yes."

"I'm Ken Somers, Kenny's son. I hope I'm not bothering you at a bad time."

"Not at all, please come in. I'm surprised to see you this morning."

"Ginny, my wife, and I spent most of the night talking. If my dad is softening a bit in his attitude, I feel I must take advantage of it. We got up around four this morning and got in the car. We just arrived in town. I have a request to make of you. May we talk?"

"Of course. Is your wife in the car? Please ask her to join us."

Ken went to his car and Christine hurried to the kitchen to put on a pot of coffee.

After introductions were made Christine asked, "How did you find me so quickly?"

"You were easy to track on the internet. I looked you up after we talked last night. I really want to see my dad. I know he may once again reject me." He paused and looked at the floor.

Ginny began to speak. "I suggested to Ken that it might be a good idea to ask you to accompany us to the home. If he rejects us again we will leave quickly and not return. But I think Kenny should have someone with him if that happens. He is bound to be upset. He seems to have made some connection with you and I think he may need a friend. If by any chance he will let Ken see him, having you there might bring them both some comfort."

"I know this is a tremendous request to make of you. But who knows how long any of us will be around?" Ken said. He looked very tired and sad.

"Ken is scheduled to go in for surgery in two days. He is having a kidney transplant. That's why we decided to come so quickly. If you feel you don't want to be a part of our effort to try to reconcile things, we certainly understand," Ginny said.

"I will do whatever I can to help you," Christine said. "Give me five minutes to change my clothes and put on some perfume." She started to laugh. "It's a game we play. I wear different perfumes and the men have to try to identify it. Help yourselves to more coffee while I make myself smell good." She hurried up the stairs.

Her mind was racing. *How can she handle this? Walk in unannounced and say 'Here is your son to see you,' in front of all his friends? Or might it be better to separate Kenny, perhaps take him outside?* That sounded better to Christine.

She made a quick call to the home to confirm that all was well with Kenny that morning and that he had no therapy or doctor visit scheduled.

As they rode together Christine began to speak.

"I often take the men outside and visit with them there. Sometimes all of them go but often I just take one at a time. There are benches among the flowers so it is a pleasant setting. Do you think it might be a nice place for you to meet or do you want to go to his room?"

"It would be nice to have a private place to meet. I wonder if he'll even see me." Ken quietly mused.

"I'll wait in the car." Ginny said. "I brought a book to read."

"I'll come out and let you know how things are going," Christine told her.

When they got to the VA Home, Christine showed Ken the path to the garden area and asked him to wait there. Then she went inside to get Kenny. She really was nervous about being a part of this yet she also felt a responsibility to make it happen.

"What are you doing here?" Bruce asked as she walked into their room. "It's not even lunch time yet."

"I missed you all so much I just had to come see you," she told them. After a few minutes of bantering about, she told Kenny she wanted to take him for a walk. He eyed her suspiciously but did not object to being pushed outside.

"I have a feeling you called my son and he told you off and now you're mad at me," Kenny said.

"I'm not mad at you Kenny, but you are right. I did call him. Your son is a very sad lonely person who needs a special man to talk with. He needs his father."

"He doesn't need me. I'd be in his way."

By this time they had reached the outside. Christine could see Ken at the end of the pathway. *It's too late to turn back now,* she thought.

"He needs you so badly that he drove all night to get here to see you this morning. He needs you more than you need him. Now be a good dad to your son."

Ken walked to the wheelchair of his father, knelt down and then put his arms around his dad. Kenny reached out to embrace his son.

Christine stepped back and watched for a moment. She felt the tears in her eyes. She left the men to go to the car to find Ginny.

Ginny started to smile as she saw Christine walking toward her. She jumped out of the car to give Christine a hug. "You did it. You did it," she cried. "Thank you, thank you, thank you."

"Let's go inside so I can introduce you to Kenny's special friends. I'm sure they've heard of you. You can see just where and how Kenny lives and reassure your Ken that his dad is doing okay," Christine told her.

"What's going on?" Mel asked as they walked into the room. "First you're here and then you're gone and now you're back with another beautiful lady."

"Mel, Bruce, Chuck, I want you to meet Kenny's daughter-in-law. This is Ginny."

Chuck spoke up. "Well, I hope this means that young Ken is outside talking to the old grouch."

"I didn't think anyone could pull this off," Bruce said. "But if anyone can do it I guess it is you, Christine."

"Do we get to meet Ken?" Mel asked.

"I'm sure they'll be in soon," she answered.

Ruth King came into the room. She introduced herself to Ginny. "Are you here for lunch?" she asked.

"Is it possible?" Christine asked.

"Absolutely," she said with a smile. "I guess there will be three more."

Christine marveled at the way Ruth seemed to grasp what was happening. She felt special to be a part of this reunion.

Kenny and Ken came in from the garden and Kenny proudly made introductions to his friends. Very quickly they all went to the dining hall. The noise of their chatter let Christine know the reconciliation had gone well and Ken and Kenny each knew he had a family. Christine began to look around the room. It was the first time she had been there for lunch.

"I don't recognize that young man sitting alone in the corner," she told Mel who was sitting next to her.

"He comes in every few months for a week or two. He lost both of his legs in a car bomb in Iraq," Mel told her.

"I think I'll go introduce myself," Christine said as she hurried away from the table.

"Hi, I'm Christine. I don't think we've met."

As he reached out to shake her hand he smiled and said, "I'm Lonny. I'm not here full time. I have to come in for a tune-up every so often then I go back home."

"With an accent like that you must be from Kentucky or nearby."

"You got it, ma'am. I come from the most beautiful horse-racing country in the world – Kentucky."

"How did you happen to settle here in California?"

"Because the most wonderful girl in the world lives here. We met when we both were on active duty in Iraq. We got married and have a little girl. When I lost both my legs we decided to come back here to be close to her family so they can help her when I'm getting treatment."

"You mentioned you're in for a tune-up. What does that mean?"

"I needed two new legs. One works just fine and gives me no trouble. The other leg – well, let's just say it needs adjustment from time to time. I come here, they fix me up, and I go home till the next time. I'll be so glad to go home. I get pretty lonely here."

"Do you have family in Kentucky?"

"Yep, a mom, dad, and brother. They work on a horse racing farm in Louisville. I really miss them. I haven't found anyone here who knows anything about horse racing."

"Well, you just sit right there. I have a friend for you to meet," Christine said as she hurried over to get Mel.

"Mel, come with me. There is someone you must meet," Christine said as she pulled him away from the table. "I'll be right back," she told the others.

As she spoke, Christine saw a somewhat anxious look on Ginny's face. She looked at Ken. He looked content yet very tired. Christine knew it was time for the visit between Kenny and his son to end, although they certainly seemed friendly. She walked with Mel to meet Lonny, hurried through the introductions, and returned to the table.

"Is it time for us to leave?" she quietly asked Ginny as she sat down beside her.

"Yes," she answered. "I can see Ken is very tired and we need to drive back home today. He's scheduled for another test early tomorrow morning."

Very smoothly Christine had them out the door and into the car.

"Why don't the two of you rest for a couple of hours at my house before you start the long drive back?" she asked.

"That's a good idea," Ginny said.

"You have many good ideas, Christine. How can we ever thank you for making today happen?" Ken asked.

"Well, maybe I'll ask you to come perform the tango for the men, Ginny. You'd look great dancing with a bowl of fruit on your head."

Their visit together sped by very quickly. They parted with promises to keep each other up-to-date on the conditions of both Ken and Kenny. Christine was so glad that Kenny had a family.

Chapter 7

Christine woke early the next morning, hurried through her exercise routine, showered and had breakfast and then sat down with all her cookbooks that featured recipes from the 1800's. Most were very basic with few frills but she had one book with food served in the homes of the very wealthy. Christine was busy making lists of the ingredients. She wanted to check to see if they were even available and that the cost of the food would be reasonable.

She was interrupted by the phone.

"Christine, this is Ruth. Am I interrupting you?"

"Not at all. It's nice to hear from you."

"I want to thank you. Not only did you help us to have a very nice Memorial Day celebration but Laura has called and offered to arrange a program for the Fourth of July. This has never happened before and I'm feeling so good about it. May I take you to lunch today to say thank you?"

"I'd love that. What time shall we meet?"

As the women sat in the Tea Room having a very pleasant lunch, Christine asked Ruth when she had started to help at the VA. Ruth said her son had been wounded in the Vietnam War and died about three months after being a patient in a VA hospital.

"I made it to the hospital in time to be with my son, but I saw many patients who died alone. I don't want that to happen to anyone if I can help. These are special men. They deserve the best."

"You are a very kind person," Christine said. "Was he your only child?"

"No, I have a daughter who has two children. She is a very kind gentle woman who works with young people. She is very concerned about the path of drugs and booze so many have chosen. She volunteers at the high school to work with the kids."

"Does she have a special concern?"

"It changes from time to time. Right now her concern is about the young people who will not be going on to college. So many schools only emphasize higher education. While that would be an ideal situation, there are many students who will not pursue that course."

"Does she have any ideas about how to change it?"

"Actually, she does. She is considering using the money she inherited from her grandmother to start training classes for young men and women to work in the food industry. Her research shows that many young people enter the restaurant business with little or no training."

"Well, I have worked in restaurants all over the United States and done just about every job you could imagine, from washing dishes and prepping food to managing service in very expensive French restaurants," Christine said with a laugh.

"I can't believe that," Ruth said with a smile.

"My first job was bussing tables when I was about five years old. My father was a coal miner in West Virginia. Right after I was born he was severely injured in a cave-in. He did not go back to the mine. The owner of the mine owned a bar in our small town. He gave my dad a job as manager of the bar. We lived in an apartment on the second floor of the building. Mom helped Dad by cooking burgers. I spent a lot of time there. I started taking dirty glasses and beer bottles to the kitchen when I was only five years old."

"Did the authorities know about it?"

"I doubt it. Usually we knew when they were coming so I'd either run upstairs to our apartment or down to the basement to hide among the supplies. It was not a bad life. The patrons were mostly locals and my dad never let anyone have too much to drink. On weekends my dad played his guitar and everyone sang along."

"Sounds like you had a good childhood."

"I have many nice memories. When I was ten my mother had another baby, a little boy. We always had a lot of music in our home even though our home was upstairs over the bar."

"How old were you when you left West Virginia?"

"Just seventeen – the day after graduation from high school. A local boy, Roger, and I got married. We headed for Nashville. Roger was sure he was the next great country-western singer. He found no job there so we left for Oklahoma. Eventually we made our way to Las Vegas. He sang for tips in various bars. I worked wherever I could find a job – kitchen help, dishwashing, prepping food, clearing tables, waitressing. I guess I've worked in almost every area of food service. I remember one time I had to fix ten different breakfasts at the same time. I learned many lessons."

"Did you always stay in that area of work?"

"I guess I did. In my so-called career in the food industry I found there are many different parts that need to be done well to be successful. You need to be able to respond to your customer – sometimes laughing and telling a joke or maybe just quietly serving a cup of tea to someone you sense is in distress. I learned many lessons the hard way."

"What was hardest for you?" Ruth asked.

Christine thought for a moment and then said, "When I was working in a sports bar in Nashville, my co-workers confronted me and told me I needed to look at my customers and be friendly and flirt a little. They said I looked down when I took orders. They told me I worried more about cleaning tables than looking at people. When I told them I thought flirting was wrong, they laughed and said it was a business tool to make customers feel good. They told me ways to keep the flirting friendly. They said my customers put very little or no tips into the jar we kept on the counter. We always split the tips. One girl told me I was costing her money and she had three kids to support. They criticized me in a soft, kind manner but I was crushed. Then they began to talk about the way

I dressed. They told me I looked very matronly. I thought I looked respectable."

"Don't most places provide uniforms of some kind?"

"Some do. At that bar we bought our own shorts but were provided with T-shirts with the bar's name on them. They suggested I exchange my extra-large T-shirts for a medium or small and buy some shorts that didn't come to my knees. I did listen to them. Once I got used to my new look, I did make friends with our regular customers. I began to enjoy my job more and I made better tips."

"How many different types of places did you work?"

"I couldn't begin to tell you – truck stops, breakfast shops, family diners, fast food places, casino bars and exclusive restaurants. I learned so much from each one. During my last years of working before I married George, I worked as a hostess and customer service manager in very expensive French restaurants in Vegas and Reno. Along the way I learned how to carve beets into beautiful red roses and other vegetables into little animals."

"I guess you need to have people skills, too."

"Most definitely. And young people especially need to know when they are being handed a line by a bad customer."

"Did you ever fall for a bad line?"

"One that still embarrasses me to this day to think about."

"Share it with me."

"Want to be in the movies?" Christine said with a smile.

"Did you fall for it?"

"I fell for it big time. It was in Vegas. My hair has always been bright red as was my father's. I inherited my pale skin from my mother. One day a man told me he was a movie producer. He said I had the skin needed for a role in a movie he was casting. But I had to dye my red hair black. I bought some black hair dye. With my pale skin I looked terrible. I looked like a ghoul. The next day everyone at worked laughed themselves silly when they saw me. When I told them why I had done it they broke into hysterical laughter again. It seems the man made horror movies. They shook their heads and laughed that I had fallen for such a stupid line. It took a lot of haircuts to get rid of the black hair. Of course the man never came back to the place."

"My daughter really needs to talk to you. I think she's serious about this program. May I ask her to call you?"

"Of course," Christine said. "I'll be happy to share what I know."

As Christine drove home she had a smile on her face. She liked having a friend with whom to share an old memory. She felt like she was really starting to make a life for herself. She didn't expect it to be the same life she had with George, nothing could match that, but now she was getting out of the house and seeing people. She was beginning to open up about her past. She had always felt so guilty and ashamed when she thought about it. *Maybe talking about it will help me get rid of those feelings.*

Life seemed to be improving for her. She was having a great deal of pleasure trying to plan the menu for the Civil War gala planned for the community. She decided to think of some ideas of costumes for the wait staff to wear. She was still planning to look for more of George's relics from the Civil War for the committee to use. She had been asked to serve on the Board of Directors at the library/museum. She enjoyed going to the VA home to visit with her friends. She was a bit concerned that the flower gardens at the VA were not as tidy as they should be. Maybe she should find time to help pull weeds. She thought about her chat with Ruth that day. She thought of a few other items that Ruth's daughter should consider if she started a program.

I think I feel stronger than I have for a long time, George. I know you're watching out for me. I'm going to be okay. Don't worry about me.

Chapter 8

*I*t's Sunday again and I'm not sure I'll go to church today, Christine thought as she came downstairs. *I must not be quite awake yet. I slept well last night, things are good in my life, yet I have this strange feeling that something is going to happen. Why do I feel this way?* She fixed some toast and coffee and sat at the kitchen table, unable to greet the day. *I guess it's because I have been so busy that I haven't been out to the rock to talk to you, George. Well, I'll fix that. As soon as church is over I'll be on my way.* As she went upstairs she noticed her mail from Saturday on the hall table. She took a moment to look through it and started to laugh.

"Now I know what's wrong. It's this letter from Mike. He's probably trying to insist that I come into his office for my annual financial check-up. We both know how much I hate doing it" she said aloud.

I know Mike's doing a good job of managing the money George left me. George trusted him and so do I. She had a bank account that always had enough money in it to cover anything she needed. She knew George was a shrewd investor and if she had any major expenses, she had money to cover it. Before he died George had tried to explain all his investments to her but she just could not get interested in it. She knew George trusted Mike, who was the son of George's good friend, Will. Will had always handled all of George's financial matters. When Will died, his son, Mike, who was an attorney, took on the job for George and then for Christine. But he had one bad habit which bothered Christine. He wanted her to read everything. She felt very confident that he would handle things wisely. She'd go in this week, look at the stack of papers briefly and tell him what a good job he was doing. She'd bake some chocolate chip cookies to take to him. Maybe he won't get so upset when she isn't interested in her financials. He had another habit which bothered her. He reminded her almost every time that if she did not make plans to spend George's money, it could revert to the state. She didn't want to think about those things.

She hurried out of church as soon as the postlude ended. No time for coffee and visiting today. She even moved a little faster to get to her car. She didn't like the sermon this morning. It really hit too close to home to make her feel good. It was about people who try to store up riches on earth instead of preparing for blessings in heaven. How timely was that? She knew she should make some decisions very soon about her small estate.

As she approached her house she saw a strange car in her driveway and people sitting on her porch. The car had license plates from Kentucky.

Whoever can that be? I don't recognize the car. It almost looks like someone is moving or living in the car. She hurried to the front porch. She saw a young couple and a baby on the swing.

"Christine?" a tall, thin young man asked her as she stepped on the porch.

"Yes," she answered. "Who are you?"

"Aunt Tina, I'm your nephew, Larry Stewart, Jr."

Christine felt like her legs had turned to rubber and she could feel her heart begin to beat rapidly. *Tina,* she thought. *I haven't been called that since I was seventeen years old. That's what my mom and dad called me.*

"I have no nephew. Who are you?"

"I'm the son of your brother Larry. I was named for my father."

"My parents and my brother were killed in a car crash many years ago," she said sternly.

"Your parents died in the accident. My dad survived the crash. He was taken in by a local family who lived in the area. He looked for you many times. He never forgot you. You were his big sister."

Time seemed to stand still. Christine felt her body start to shake. She thought she might fall down so she reached out to hold onto the railing that surrounded the porch. *Who is this stranger? Am I really hearing what happened to my family? Is he really my nephew or someone trying to scam me?*

"Is he alive now? Where is he?" Christine asked.

"He died last year."

Is this really true? This man called me Tina. That's what my family called me. No one had used that name in years. Was my brother really alive all those years? At first Christine said nothing. She was stunned and confused. She became aware of the woman and child on the swing.

"This must be your family," she finally said.

"Aunt Tina, meet my wife, Jody, and daughter, Bella."

The young woman had been sitting there with her head bent over her daughter. She looked up shyly and said, "Hi."

There were so many questions Christine wanted to ask. Was he really her nephew? She thought about how gullible she had been about people in her early life. She had vowed never to be so trusting again. But if he really is her nephew it would be wonderful. George was the only family she had since she was seventeen years old. And now he was gone.

How do you begin? At what point in time do you start asking questions Christine wondered. She heard the baby start to awaken and fuss a little. Memories of her baby, the one she had never had a chance to hold, flooded her mind. She saw a beautiful little girl with little ringlets of gold hair on her head. She looked like a happy healthy baby. *Is this my great-niece,* she thought? *How can I really be sure that this man is who he says he is?*

Saying a quick, silent prayer asking God to keep her safe, she said, "Let's go in the house. We have many, many things to talk about. Have you had lunch?" she asked.

"I know our visit comes as a shock to you," Larry said quietly. "If you don't feel comfortable asking us in your house, we can arrange to meet somewhere."

"Of course we'll go in," Christine said as she unlocked the door. "Come in and sit down while I put the coffee on.

We can talk all afternoon." She indicated they should sit in the family room that adjoined the kitchen.

Jody took a blanket from the diaper bag and spread it on the floor. She put the baby on the blanket and then took some baby food from the bag and began to feed Bella.

Christine looked at them and thought they made a beautiful picture of a family. One she never got to experience. Her lingering doubts began to dim. There was something very familiar about Larry. She couldn't quite place what it was – his mannerisms, the way he used his hands to make a point seemed to resonate with her. He did call her *Tina*. Only her immediate family called her that. She had never told anyone about that name. He sounded very sincere when he talked.

Jody remained very quiet as she looked after the baby.

Christine went to her freezer and removed three individual chicken casseroles and put them in the microwave oven to heat. She made coffee and fixed a salad and set the table. The baby quickly went to sleep after being fed so the three of them had a quiet meal together.

"How did you finally locate me?" Christine asked as they finished eating.

"Through the use of the internet. It helps you locate anyone. Dad remembered that you married Roger Parker so I started to look for a Christine Parker. I found a Christine and Roger Parker in Las Vegas who had gotten a divorce who were the right age. I checked marriage license records and found you had married a man named Martinelli. I learned Mr. Martinelli had died. After checking around a bit more I found your work record at a French restaurant in Vegas. I contacted them and was told you had transferred to Reno. Jody and I had decided to leave Kentucky when I was offered a job in Seattle. We decided to travel through Reno to try to find you. At the French restaurant in Reno, someone remembered you had married a man named George McCall and moved here to Crofton. We thought that since we were so close and could travel to Seattle this way that we'd try to find you. I hope your husband won't mind us stopping by unannounced."

"My husband has been gone for five years now," Christine told him. "But before we talk about the past, let me ask about you two and the baby."

Jody had not uttered a word since the first "Hi" when they were introduced. She kept her head down and only looked up when she checked on the baby who was sound asleep on the floor.

"Jody and I have been together for almost five years now. Little Bella was a very pleasant surprise but one we were not quite ready for. I worked in construction back home. I heard about a lot of building going on in the Seattle area so we decided to try for a new start out there. It was a lot farther and a bit harder to get this far than I thought it would be, but I know we'll be OK when we get to Seattle." He paused and then continued. "Do you know of a small motel close by where we can stay tonight? The engine on my car is making a funny noise and I need to get it checked out before we leave here. I don't want to have a breakdown on the highway."

"You must stay here, of course. We have many things to talk about. I want to know as much as I can about my parent's and my brother's last days. I have a guest room you can use. It's possible that George's old crib and highchair are up in the attic. He grew up in this house and his mother saved everything. We'll check it out later. What do you think, Jody? Does that sound OK?"

"That sounds wonderful," Larry answered for Jody. "We've had a hard trip."

"Then let me clear the table and make a fresh pot of coffee. Then we'll talk."

Larry began to speak. "My dad talked very little about his early life. He was a very quiet man with few friends. He grew up in the foster care system in Kentucky and was on his own by the time he was sixteen. He married my mother who died when I was born. He lived in his own world as an auto mechanic. I pretty much grew up on my own. He made me go to school and learn a trade. When I questioned him about his parents he only talked about it once. When I pressed him for more information, he wouldn't talk about it. But he did talk about you, Aunt Tina. He said you were beautiful and used to read to him. He remembered you reading *The Little Engine That Could*. He always remembered that story."

Christine felt the tears begin to well in her eyes. She remembered so well getting that book from the library time after time. Together they said the words, "*I think I can, I think I can.*" Finally for his birthday one year she had bought the book for him. That's not the kind of information you get from the internet.

"Did he remember anything about the accident?" she asked.

"Not too much. Dad told me that his parents missed you so much after you left that they decided to leave West Virginia and move to Nashville to be close to you. The car was packed with all their belongings. They were going to take turns driving and not stop at night. Dad was asleep in the back seat when the car apparently went off the road on a dark rainy night. Dad was only seven years old at the time. He woke up to find his parents dead. There seemed to be no other traffic around. He was never sure how long he waited there for help to arrive. Finally he made his way up a hillside to the highway. Eventually he was picked up and taken to the nearest town. He was put into the foster care system. Dad didn't talk about that period of time."

"Did the authorities ever find the car? Were my parents buried in the area?"

"Dad was always very vague about it. He got a sad look on his face and his hands would start to shake. As a child I learned not to ask him about it."

"Do you know where this accident happened?"

"No, I don't know. He never said. He only said he had lived in every small town in western West Virginia and eastern Kentucky."

Christine sat quietly trying to absorb all this news. *Why wasn't I stronger? Why did I let anyone tell me I must marry Roger Parker? My parents might have had many happy years together if I had stayed home. I might have grown up knowing my little brother.* Christine became aware of the tears that were flowing down her cheeks.

Quietly she reached for a tissue. "At last I know what happened."

Jody went to the kitchen and brought Christine a cup of coffee.

Christine showed them to the guest bedroom and asked Larry to go with her to the attic where they found the crib and highchair used by George so many years ago. They were covered with a drop cloth and then a sheet of plastic and looked almost like new as they were uncovered. Larry carried them downstairs. After the baby was put to bed for the night, Christine could feel her body start to shake. She was torn between happiness at learning she had a family yet realized these people might not be truthful. She left them at a fairly early hour and went to bed.

George, I don't know what to do, she thought. *I want to believe that Larry is really my nephew. I want and need a family. I miss you so much to help me figure out if I am really hearing the truth. I don't know what questions to ask to be sure. I really want to believe I now have a family.* She sat quietly for a few minutes, and then picked up George's picture from her nightstand. "I'm sorry, George, that I didn't get out to the rock today to talk with you," she said quietly. "I guess I'll just have to take one day at a time. I'm glad Larry is going to take his car in for repairs tomorrow and then maybe they'll be on their way. It will give me time to figure out what to do." She turned off her bedside light. She said a quick prayer asking God to help her make good decisions. She had a restless night full of dreams.

Chapter 9

The next day after Larry had gone to the garage, Christine tried to make friends with Jody. It was not easy. Jody answered each question very politely but never initiated any conversation. Jody appeared to be a good mother to little Bella, making sure she was clean and safe and not hungry, but she did not cuddle the baby or talk to her in front of Christine. Christine asked Jody about baby food and diapers, and as Christine suspected, was told that Jody had no supply of either.

"Come with me. We'll go to the store to get what you need," Christine volunteered.

Jody fastened the baby into the car seat that doubled as a carrier. It looked very flimsy to Christine. She thought she had heard something about special car seats to secure in the car, but she decided to say nothing. After all, she hadn't been around a baby for years and years. What did she know? They went to the local Target store. When Jody expressed a word of concern about the money to pay for the items they bought, Christine told her not to worry because they were family. Christine watched

Jody as she tried to decide which new outfit Christine insisted on buying for the baby. *I wonder how old Jody is. She can't be any older than sixteen or seventeen and maybe not that old. Yet Larry says they have been together for almost five years.*

When they got home, Christine began to take care of little Bella. The baby laughed and cooed and cuddled against Christine's breast. Christine fell in love with this sweet baby.

Larry arrived home with the news that his car needed a special part that had to be sent from San Francisco. It would take a few days. "Sorry to ask you this, Aunt Tina, but do you think we could stay for another couple of days?"

"Of course, you can," Christine told him. "I may never let this baby out of my sight. But would you please bring downstairs the rocking chair from my bedroom so that I can rock her?"

Christine thought she saw a moment of pain come over Jody's face, but Jody said nothing. *Maybe she thinks the baby will grow close to me,* Christine thought.

That night Christine decided to ask more questions about her brother: how tall he was – the same height as Larry; did his hair ever turn from blond to red – it did not. Larry did say his father remembered how Christine took care of him while his mother worked in the bar below the apartment where they lived. Her brother had apparently told his son about Christine running to hide when the state and county officials came by the bar. He remembered about Christine being called "Little Red."

When Christine went to bed that night she knew she was becoming convinced that these people who had come to her home really were her family.

The next day Larry decided to try to find work for a couple of days while he waited for the car repair to be made. He left early in the morning and they didn't see him all day. He came home smiling with $80 in his hand that he had made that day. He repeated the process each of the next few days.

Christine decided she needed to keep up with her usual routine so she made some spaghetti and fixed a salad to take to her friends at the retirement village. Ed and Henry were glad to see her but questioned her about why she had left church so suddenly on Sunday. "Was she sick?" they asked. After all, they had promised George to look after her.

She assured them she was fine and then left to deliver food to Ron Davis who lived in a separate building.

"Ron, I'm not sure I'm going to be able to make it out to the VA nursing center this week. I've had unexpected company. Very unexpected."

"Is that good or bad news?" he asked her. "Why don't you come in? You look a bit troubled. Let me get you a cup of coffee."

Christine stepped inside.

"I think it's good. I thought my parents and brother had been killed in a car accident many, many years ago. I have just learned my brother was not killed. He died not too long ago. His son showed up on my doorstep on Sunday with his wife and child. They'll be leaving again by the end of the week and I want to spend time with them."

"Did you even know about them?" Ron asked.

"No. It was a total surprise."

"Are you feeling any reason to doubt that he is who he says he is?"

"Part of my brain is telling me that after nearly forty years of thinking I had no living relatives I now have a family. But another part of my brain is telling me that it's not possible that these people are for real. Then I see some motions or movements Larry makes that seem familiar to me. He has talked about a few things from my early life that I don't think anyone else would know." Christine paused and took a sip of her coffee. Then she continued.

"Ron, I don't know how much you know about my past, but before I met George I trusted everyone and made many, many wrong decisions. A bit of my brain is telling me to be careful but another part of my brain is telling me I now have a family. Their baby is so beautiful. She has wrapped her little fingers around my heart."

Ron sat quietly listening and then he spoke.

"Christine, are you aware that before I retired I had my own investigation firm? I did mostly corporate work but I have many contacts I could call on to confirm your nephew's story. I'll be glad to do so."

"It seems rather sleazy and unkind to do that. He'll probably be gone in a day or so and I won't hear from him again."

"Well, think on it. It won't cost anything just to ask a few questions."

Christine went home with a lot on her mind. Larry informed her that the car part sent from San Francisco was the wrong part but the correct part had been re-ordered.

As Christine played with little Bella and rocked her to sleep that night, she had feelings of ownership for the baby. *This is my brother's little granddaughter. I must take care of her forever. I must do this for my brother Larry.*

A few more days passed. It was time for Christine to meet with Mike about the financial affairs. Maybe now she might have someone to name in a will. She still had moments of doubt about Larry. Jody didn't talk about anything. But sweet little Bella had nothing but coos and smiles for Christine.

"How are you, Christine?" Mike asked as she entered the lawyer's office.

"Maybe a little better than I thought I'd be. You know how much I detest talking about money."

"Somehow I get that idea when I have to beg you to come in to discuss it," Mike said. "Do you want some coffee?" he asked. When she said she did not, with a smile he said, "Are you trying to bribe me with chocolate chip cookies?"

"Me? Do that?" she asked with a smile.

"Of course you would. And I will eat every one of them. But let's get busy." He had folders in front of him which he began to open.

Christine sat quietly for a minute or so, not looking at the papers. She looked at Mike and very seriously asked, "Did your father ever tell you anything about my past life before I met George?"

"He did not, but based on my experience with people, I guess that you worked very hard to earn a living. Most people who do so usually are reluctant to discuss money. And I certainly know how reluctant you are," he said with a smile.

"You're right. George changed my life in so many ways. I was totally alone in the world when I met him. I had no relatives or close friends. After we married I knew that George had invested wisely. We seemed to need so little money to live on. We had enough to travel and do what we wanted to do. Neither of us had a family to inherit his estate." She paused and then continued. "Many, many years ago I was informed that my parents and little brother were killed in a car crash when I was just seventeen years old. I had already married and left home. I had no other family." She paused and then added, "Well, at least that's what I thought. I had a surprise waiting for me when I got home from church on Sunday. My brother, Larry, whom I thought was killed in a car crash when he was seven years old, actually survived for many years. Apparently he told his son about me, his sister. The son, Larry Junior, began an internet search for me and turned up on my doorstep on Sunday with his wife and baby."

Christine saw Mike's eyes widen with surprise.

"Do you believe he is who he says he is?"

"I didn't at first but he has told me things that are helping to change my mind. I've heard that lawyers are always skeptical. I can tell from the look on your face that you are leery about him."

"Forgive me, Christine, if I'm not enthusiastic about long lost relatives appearing on the doorstep of a rich aunt.

George made my dad promise to look out for you. As my dad lay dying he passed that responsibility to me. It's one I gladly accepted. But Christine, con men are everywhere. Do you have any idea of the amount of your estate?"

"I know I have enough to live on very, very comfortably. Until now I didn't know what I would do if there was anything left over. Just plan an expensive funeral, I guess."

"Then plan for a very expensive funeral," Mike told her. He opened a folder and placed it in front of her. "Just look at the bottom line. Don't just close your eyes and tell me everything looks fine like you usually do. Really look at it."

Christine's eyes opened wide when she really saw the amount. "There must be some mistake, there are too many zero's on the amount."

"No, Christine, there are no mistakes. George was a shrewd investor, spreading his money in various accounts. He also left behind five different parcels of land around the country. Three of them were sold for a very big profit. You spend practically nothing to live on. The amount of your estate continues to grow."

Christine continued to look at the amount. She could only count zeroes. Finally she looked up and said, "That's more than a million dollars. I had no idea my reserve money was anything that large. I thought maybe a few thousand.

Mike smiled at her and said, "Much more than a million. Now maybe you will understand why my dad and I tried to insist you become more aware of the amount. You've given us a very hard time."

"George was so good to me. He said he'd take care of me forever."

"George was a very good man. He really loved you, Christine. I hope you'll now understand my skepticism about long lost relatives who appear."

"But how would anyone know about it?" Christine asked.

"The internet. The same internet that helped your so-called nephew find you. A skilled user can find out almost anything about a person. It's easy for someone to get a few basic facts and try to pull a scam."

"But Larry knew things about my childhood: how as a child I worked in the bar my father managed, and a favorite book I read to his father. He knows all about my early years. He even calls me 'Aunt Tina.' No one knew that my folks called me "Tina" except a few people in West Virginia fifty years ago."

"He may be legit, Christine. I wish you hadn't let him in your house until we had checked him out."

"Ron Davis said the same thing. I took him some spaghetti when I took some to Ed and Henry yesterday.

"Dad always loved your pasta when you brought it to him. You were a good friend to Dad and his friends. I think Ron is right. Why don't you let him do a bit of investigating to see if Larry Junior is really who he says he is? Ron is very intelligent and always operates very low-key so that no one knows what he's doing. Could I give him a call to see if he can talk with us now so that we can make a plan? Trying to keep this so-called nephew from scamming you for your money is one thing, but your safety is another. I don't think we should waste any time."

"Well, if you think it's best, I guess it's OK." she said slowly.

Ron arrived in less than twenty minutes.

"I'm glad Christine told you about her so-called nephew," Ron said when he came in the office. "I know you want to believe he is a relative, and maybe he is, Christine, but there are so many con men out there it's a smart thing to confirm to be sure."

"Do you have any ideas how to proceed to find out?" Mike asked Ron.

"Well, I'd say DNA is the best way to be sure. I have some kits at home. I have a private lab I use for analysis which should get us results in two or three days. If we find out they are a match we can all relax and you can enjoy your new-found family. Do you want to go home and ask him to provide a sample?"

"I keep thinking about that sweet little baby," Christine said. "What if he doesn't want to provide a sample? What if I find out he's really my nephew? I'll have to live remembering that I didn't really trust him. What if he is a scammer? What will happen to the baby?"

"There are ways I can get a sample without arousing suspicions. Serve him a bottle of beer. I can get a sample from that. If it shows he's a relative he will never know you checked on him."

Christine thought about it. She sat with her head bowed trying to decide.

Mike spoke up. "Maybe I'm making too much of all this. But in my experience handling estates, I have had many phony relatives appear when money is involved.

Maybe I've said too much and raised too much doubt. But I must be certain that you are safe." He could see how troubled Christine was.

"Usually," Ron began, "I don't do DNA tests until I've done a bit of investigation first. Maybe if I do some investigation along with the DNA test we'd all be a bit more comfortable. Christine, I have found you to be a smart, intelligent, intuitive woman. When I took you to the VA home you immediately knew how to react to each person's needs. What is your gut feeling about young Larry? Down deep do you really believe him?"

Christine thought before she answered.

"I never knew what happened to my parents and brother. I left home when I was seventeen years old and never heard another word from them. Down deep in my soul I know I want to believe that he is family. But in my past life, before George, I made many mistakes when I was too trusting of people. I vowed never to trust anyone again. George helped me to believe in myself. But I always knew I had him by my side. I just wish I had him here to help make the decision." She paused. "I suppose it's the right thing to do."

"Christine, I feel certain that this is the path George would want you to take. He hated fakes and phonies. He admired your ability to see things as they are and not what you want them to be," Mike said as he came and put his arms around her.

Mike turned to Ron and said, "Be very careful not to let him get suspicious and put Christine in harm's way."

"I'll do my very best," Ron said as he turned to Christine. "Why don't we go somewhere for coffee and you can tell me about your family. I'll see if I can find anything on the internet this afternoon. Invite me for dinner tonight. I'll bring the beer. Don't offer him a glass for his beer; I'll get a better sample from the bottle than I can get from a glass. Maybe we can get all this over with in a couple of days and you can relax and enjoy your new family."

Mike spoke up. "I'd like to be part of the conversation. Why don't we step into the conference room? We'll have more space there. There may be some way I can help legally to solve this mystery."

He rang for his secretary and told her they were going to the conference room and to cancel his plans for that morning. When the secretary brought them a tray of coffee he told her he was not to be disturbed.

"Let's start with your dad and mom. When did you last see them?" Ron began to enter information on his laptop computer. "Where did he work? Was he a professional man?"

"No, he was a coal miner until he was injured. Then he managed a bar in a little town in West Virginia. I lived with my mother and dad upstairs over the bar until I left home when I was seventeen."

"If he was a coal miner then he must have belonged to a union. I'll check West Virginia union records. You said he was injured. Did he get a disability income? It's another way to check. Did your mother have your brother at home or in a hospital? Do you remember the make and color of the car? When did you last hear from them? Was it a friendly parting?"

Mike spoke. "You said you were very young when you left home. Were you following a dream or was there family trouble that made you leave home so early?"

Christine paused with her head down and then began to speak. "I guess I'd have to say both reasons, though it was not my dream. The community I lived in was very small. Roger's parents were almost non-existent so he spent a lot of time at our house. He and my dad would sit in the bar and play guitars and sing together. Roger was sure he was the world's greatest country-western singer. Roger and I were the only two students of high school age. Rather than pay for a school bus, the officials paid for the gas for Roger to drive us both to school each day. On the night of our senior banquet, Roger pulled into a dark, secluded area." She paused, looked at both Mike and Ron. "No, we did not have sex. But maybe Roger did want to. He got very physical. I might not have known what I wanted in life but I had absolutely no feelings at all for Roger. I began to fight him off. Just then the car door opened and I saw my dad. I thought I was rescued from Roger. I was wrong. My dad assumed that we had been having sex. He thought I might already be pregnant. He insisted we had to get married right away. I couldn't understand this attitude from my dad for he was a loving father. I felt I had let him down. Roger and I both graduated the next day and then headed for a Justice of the Peace and were married. Almost immediately we left for Nashville. We had $100 and an old car. But Roger's dream was to be famous."

Mike poured a cup of coffee for Christine and asked her to continue with the story.

"We lived in the car. I used gas station restrooms for bathing and laundry. We made it to Nashville. When we stopped at truck stops he'd always take his guitar in with him and try to earn a few tips singing for the travelers. I let him make all the decisions. Roger didn't get a job or any recognition in Nashville. He said we were leaving for Oklahoma City. Many famous singers got their start there. I can remember getting so fed up with our life style I wanted to get a job to try to save some money for the trip. Roger slapped me hard and told him he would make all the decisions for our life. I was stunned and shocked. My father had treated my mom and me as ladies. Except for his fury when he found me in the car I had never seen him really angry. We headed for Oklahoma.

"While traveling, a line of tornadoes moved into the area. We stopped at a truck stop for shelter until the weather improved. Many other people had also stopped there. The restaurant was very, very crowded. The people stopping by looked tired and worried. Roger began entertaining the people with his tip jar by his side. I saw the wait staff was totally swamped. I began to pick up dirty dishes and take them to the kitchen. The cook just looked at me, gave me a spray bottle with disinfectant in it and a roll of paper towels. I cleaned tables for almost two hours. After the storm passed the cook asked me if I had eaten that day. I told him I had not. He filled a bag with sandwiches and hot soup and sent us on our way."

"Did Roger find success in Oklahoma City?" Ron asked.

"Of course not. We moved on to Vegas. But he had new rules for me. I was to get a job to keep food on the table. I had no trouble getting a job in Vegas. But I was weary of Roger and his controlling life style. He demanded on using my tip money for new clothes for his performances. He did get a job singing each night in a very small bar. He sang for tip money." Christine paused, then continued. "By this time I hated Roger and everything about our life. I decided I had to change something. I began to save half of my tip money. I wanted to return to West Virginia. I had not heard anything from my parents all this time because we didn't stay in one place long enough to get mail."

"I bet Larry found your savings that you hid on a cupboard shelf," Ron said.

"You're right, although it was hidden in a dresser drawer. But I was getting a little self-respect back so started to save again. This time I kept the money in the shoes I wore each day and I didn't let the shoes out of my sight. Roger worked nights and I worked days. We seldom saw each other. One evening I discovered some sexy underwear. I left work early the next day, came home to find Roger in bed with a young girl." Christine had a half smile on her face as she continued. "I guess I really scared them. They both ran out to the street wearing nothing. I threw their clothes out after them. The next morning I got in the car with all my clothes and headed for West Virginia. I wanted my parents. I wanted my brother. And yes, I also wanted to see the beautiful hills of my home state."

Mike and Ron began laughing as they pictured the scene that took place.

"Way to go, Christine," Mike said as he laughed.

"I bet Roger will never forget that. Had you saved enough money for the trip? Were your folks glad to see you?" Ron asked.

"I found my hometown very deserted. I went to the bar where my father worked. It was a mess; dirty both inside and out and very few light bulbs working. I was afraid my father must be very ill. A stranger was tending bar. When I asked if Red was there (Red was my dad) he didn't even know who Red was. A man sitting at the very dark bar recognized me.

"Aren't you Red's daughter,' he asked me.

"I said I was and asked if he knew where I could find him. No one was able help me. My family always kept to themselves and I knew very few people. I thought about Roger's parents so drove there. The place was overgrown with weeds. I found his father, probably drunk, asleep on an old sofa that was on the front porch. He had no idea where my folks might be and said his wife had left him. He didn't ask a thing about Roger."

"Were you able to find out what happened to them," Mike asked.

"No. I finally went to a woman who had owned a small café down the street. She was a kind, gentle person who told me my parents had left town to make their way to Nashville. They said they missed me. Then she quietly told me that while she knew nothing for certain there had been rumors that my family was involved in a car accident and all had died." Christine felt her body tense up as she told the story. It was hard for her to continue.

"I'll probably never forget that day. I had never felt so alone. I had an old car that made a lot of noise, and less than $50 in my purse and no where to go."

"What did you do?" Mike said.

"I left town and drove until I found a motel with rooms for $8 a night, got some coffee and went to the room to cry. The next morning I got a job as a cook in a diner. As soon as I saved enough money to go to the next town I left. Then I repeated my steps to get to the next town on my way to trace their route to Nashville."

Finally, very quietly, Ron asked. "Were you able to confirm their death?"

"No. I searched accident records in every city or big town between home and Nashville. But I found no records of them. George asked an investigator to look into it when we got married but he wasn't able to find any trace of them."

"So much information is available on the Internet now," Ron said.

He continued to ask Christine questions and entered the information into the computer. Her father was a miner so he started to check union records. He was injured on disability. He checked those records. Did she remember the make of the car he was driving? Ron asked her many questions.

Mike also began to ask her questions, "Aside from the fact that you have no proof they are dead or alive, what makes you think this man calling himself Larry might be legitimate?"

"He knew so many little things. From the time I was five or six years old, I cleared tables in the bar. He knew how I ran and hid in the basement or upstairs where we lived when the state inspectors came by. He knew how I used to spend hours reading to my brother. He even knew our favorite book, *The Little Engine That Could,* and how we chanted together, '*I think I can! I think I can!*' But there is more than that. Sometimes the way he tilts his head in a peculiar way seems familiar." Christine looked very puzzled and worried as she talked.

Mike and Ron then took turns questioning her about her past and the story that Larry Junior had told her about her brother. Had he showed her any pictures or mementos from the past?

The questions flowed from the two men. Christine revealed those facts about her early life that she had last spoken to George all those years ago. It was painful for her yet she felt a kind of relief that maybe now she might learn what had happened.

Finally, Ron said he had enough information to start a search.

As Christine turned to leave the office she turned to Mike and Ron and said, "I know George must be smiling down from heaven right now to know that such good people are helping me."

Chapter 10

Christine had very mixed feelings as she left the office. On one hand she felt she was being disloyal to her brother by checking on his son. On the other hand she felt she should protect the estate George left her. It was not her money. It was earned and invested by George. She was still in shock as she considered the amount; she had no idea it had grown so much since George had died. It was true, she spent very little. But she didn't need to spend money. She already had all she needed. She worried about how she would get through dinner. What could she cook for dinner that goes with beer? She had a few steaks in the freezer. Maybe she'd ask Larry to cook them on the grill. Ron and Larry could have a beer and chat while the steaks cooked. Christine always felt better when she was around the kitchen so she began to feel more confident about getting through the evening.

Jody was in the kitchen heating up some soup when Christine arrived home for lunch.

"I thought maybe soup might be OK," she said quietly.

"That's a wonderful idea. It will taste good. I always hate business meetings and this morning was no different.

I'm glad to be home. And where is my precious baby," she said looking around.

"I think I just heard her wake up," Jody said. "I'll get her."

It was the first time, maybe ever, that Christine had come home and found food ready to eat. How nice it would be if these people really are relatives. In her mind she could see birthdays and holidays shared with family. *I do so hope they are my family,* she thought. When Jody carried the baby back into the kitchen the baby looked at Christine and reached out her little arms. Christine took the baby and held her close. *How can I doubt that this baby is part of my family? I can never let her go.*

Christine decided she needed to try to get Jody to talk about her past.

"Did you always live in Kentucky?" she asked Jody.

"Yes."

"I bet your folks hated to see you leave. Did you come from a large family?"

"No."

"No brothers or sisters I guess."

There was no answer but Christine was not ready to give up.

"I bet your mom and dad hated to see you leave with little Bella." Christine waited for an answer but instead Jody picked up the baby.

"It's time for her nap. I'll put her down now."

"Well, if she goes down quickly come back down so we can get better acquainted. I'd like to know all about you."

"Okay," Jody said. But she did not return downstairs until the baby woke up a few hours later.

Such a quiet young woman. I bet she's had a hard past. Maybe she was kicked out by her parents for getting pregnant when she wasn't married. Christine had worked with the public for so many years she thought she was good about drawing people out of their shell, but nothing seemed to work with Jody.

Christine went to the kitchen, made a couple of fruit pies, took the steaks from the freezer, and started to prepare dinner. Larry got home about five o'clock in a good mood. He had found another day job and had earned another $80. He said he had stopped by the garage and found the part for his car had arrived from San Francisco. The garage had promised to get started on the repair first thing in the morning.

"I don't want to hear that," Christine said. "We're just starting to get acquainted."

"We've bothered you enough. It's time we get on our way. How did your business meeting go today?" Larry asked.

"It's always the same thing. I look at a lot of papers that I don't understand and then initial them and come home. George took care of business for me."

"He must have been a good man. Are you seeing anyone since his death?"

Christine almost started to shout 'of course not' but then thought about Ron coming for dinner.

"My heart belongs to George forever but I have many men friends. One of them, Ron Davis, is coming for dinner. He said he is anxious to meet someone from my family. I hope you will like him. I thought we'd cook out steaks and maybe eat out on the patio. Does that sound OK to you?" Christine's heart was pounding. She wasn't used to this kind of plotting.

"I'll be happy to meet him," Larry said.

When the doorbell rang, Christine heard Larry go to the door.

"You must be Aunt Tina's friend, Ron. I'm her nephew, Larry. Please come in."

"Nice to meet you, Larry. I'm glad to meet some of Christine's family."

"It's nice to have two big strong men here who know just how to cook a steak," Christine said as she greeted Ron. "How's your family?" she asked Ron as if they were long time friends.

Ron played along. "They said to say Hi and hope you'll be able to come to dinner soon."

Christine felt her legs shaking. *I'll never be able to get through this evening. This feels dishonest to me. Yet I really don't know either Larry or Ron very well. I'll postpone making any decisions about whether to go ahead with an investigation until tomorrow morning. Things are moving too fast,* she thought.

"Something sure smells good here in the kitchen," Ron said. "I brought some beer for us to enjoy while the steaks cook. Or do you prefer wine?" he asked Larry.

"Beer will be fine," Larry said as he opened two bottles.

"Are you a sports fan, Larry?" Christine heard Ron ask as the men headed outside with the steaks. It appeared that the conversation was going well. Jody brought little Bella downstairs, who as usual was all smiles for Christine. They made their way out to the patio.

Christine was sure she would not make it through the dinner without saying something wrong, but baby Bella took care of her concerns. The baby laughed and cooed and reached out for Ron to take her.

"She knows that I'm a grandpa," he said as he took her. "How is it that little girls can be so smart?"

"She's a beauty all right and we love her," Larry said.

Christine glanced at Jody and was surprised to see a look of disbelief or terror come over her face. Or maybe she just imagined it in her nervous condition. "Why don't you move to the chairs while I clear the table?" she asked.

"Christine tells me you have car problems," she heard Ron say as they left the table. She knew Ron would try to keep him busy so she could remove Larry's beer bottle to a safe place for testing. She carefully placed it in a paper bag which she set inside her cupboard. She saw the men go to the car and look it over. Jody had taken the baby back upstairs.

Christine wondered how she could get through the next hour, or the next day or the next whatever. She wondered if anyone else noticed her hands shaking. Then she noticed that Ron was watching her. He gave her a slight motion with a small wave of his fingers to try to reassure her.

"I wonder if I might go upstairs and say goodnight to Jody and the baby?" Ron asked. "After that most delicious dinner I'm afraid I'll go to sleep if I sit in that big chair," he added with a smile.

"I'll go get her," Larry said as he left the room.

Ron became all business the minute Larry left the room.

"Listen carefully and don't let on what I'm saying," Ron began. "I have already confirmed that your father is dead. I am now tracing where he is buried. That should help get us information on your mother and brother. I expect to have that news tonight or tomorrow. Give me the beer bottle before I leave. If you need to, say it is a gift for my daughter. Try to find a way we can get the baby alone. I want to do a DNA test on her. Do you have a lock on your bedroom door? If not, brace it with a chair tonight. Keep your cell phone on you at all times and keep my phone number on speed dial." As he talked with her he quickly reached into his pocket. "Open your mouth so I can get your DNA."

He made one quick swipe in her jaw with something that looked like a Q-tip. He smiled and said "I guess that didn't hurt too much."

"You mean you got it that quickly?" she asked.

"That's all there is to it. Now we can learn whether or not Larry is your blood relative."

He saw her startled and worried look.

"Sorry, Christine, all this talk has to be making you nervous. I guess I'm getting overly protective. I'm sure you'll be fine. I'll call you first thing in the morning."

Larry brought little Bella downstairs. She reached out for Ron who took her, cuddled her and returned her to Larry. Then he left.

Christine knew she was going to have a restless night. What had she gotten herself into? She picked up George's picture, held it close to her bosom, and sat on the side of the bed. She seemed to feel him sitting beside her, putting his arms around her. She knew she would be okay.

Early the next morning Christine called Ron to let him know she was fine and she had a plan. Why doesn't he stop by this morning? She'd try to get Jody out of the house to buy a new pair of jeans and he can baby sit with Bella.

He agreed to do so.

Larry left the house to do whatever it was he was doing each day. Ron arrived around 9:30.

"I would like to repay you for last night's dinner by taking you all out for lunch today," Ron said as he came in the door.

"Larry is already gone for the day but I think that sounds very nice. What do you think, Jody?"

"You two go. I'll stay here with the baby."

"No, I insist," Ron said with authority. "We'll go to a family friendly place and show off your beautiful daughter."

"Do we need to buy more diapers for the baby?" Christine asked.

"I'll send Larry tonight for more," Jody answered.

"Nonsense. I won't take no for an answer. Ron, you can baby sit long enough for us to shop, can't you? I want to buy something special for Jody. She is my niece and will be leaving soon." She turned to Jody. "Let me buy you something, maybe a new dress or jeans and a new top."

Christine had guessed that Jody had only two pairs of jeans, both of which were frayed and worn. She hoped Jody would take the bait. And she did.

"Larry will be very mad at me when he comes home," she told Christine.

"Oh, don't worry about that. I'll tell him I insisted. Maybe I'll take him out to buy a new pair of jeans." Christine spoke with more bravado than she felt. She had become aware that Larry seemed to want to keep Jody under his control. She hoped that Larry wouldn't take out his anger on Jody and hurt her. But Christine felt this was a risk she must take.

Ron spoke. "Christine, we don't want to upset Larry. Let's do this. Let's all drive to the store and I'll stay in the car with Bella while you shop. Then we'll all go for lunch."

"That's a wonderful plan," Christine said. "Let's go."

"Let's take my car. I've got a baby car seat that I use for my grandkids. Bella will be safe," Ron said.

Christine could see a look of fear come over Jody's face. *She's afraid of something. Is she afraid of Larry?* Christine wondered.

Jody finally said she'd go shopping with them. She seemed very young and excited to be going to shop for something for her.

With only one quick stop for Ron to drop off a small package at one of the office buildings, they made their way to the mall. Jody got more and more excited as they reached the store. Once inside, she seemed to know exactly what she wanted. When she tried on the jeans, she became interested in the clothes and how they fit her young body. She acted like an experienced shopper in some ways, but seemed like a young teenager in others. Christine wondered what had happened to this young girl to make her feel and act like an old woman most of the time. Jody was a young, bright beautiful teen-ager. Christine felt very puzzled about the transformation.

After a very nice lunch that the baby slept through, Ron drove them home. Jody immediately took the baby upstairs.

"Did you get a chance to get what you needed for the DNA test?" Christine asked Ron.

"I did it while you two were talking. It's just a swab in her cheek. I dropped it off at the lab on our way to the restaurant."

"Why did you want to test the baby? Is there something you know that you haven't told me?"

"Sometimes an old experienced investigator like me just gets a hunch about something. I don't know where it will lead but it will bother me like an itch that won't go away. I usually just follow through on it. Sometimes it proves to be nothing, other times it proves helpful."

"Well," Christine began, "I don't know how I'll ever be able to thank you enough. As nervous as I am, I feeling so much safer with you checking things out."

"I'm going to leave now, but stay alert. Larry may be very unhappy about your shopping trip."

As soon as Larry came in the door Christine went on the offensive.

'Larry, I know you, Jody, and Bella will be leaving soon so I had to take action today. Ron came by to take us to lunch and while we were out I bought Jody a new outfit. Consider it a going away present. Now I'd like to buy you something. Maybe you'd like a new jacket or perhaps new jeans? Moving to Seattle will take a lot of your money to get settled. Please let me do this for my family."

Larry looked very disturbed when Christine began to talk, but simply said "Thank you for the gifts for Jody but I don't need a thing."

Christine smoothly began to talk about preparing dinner.

Chapter 11

R on hurried home from Christine's house. He hoped some of the information he had sent for had arrived. He was having very uneasy feelings about the whole bit of relatives. He wished that Larry and his family were at a motel instead of her house. But he had to admit it felt good to be back in the investigation business again. He had only had one case since he sold his company but from time to time he and other retired investigators helped each other with some investigation. This is what he was depending on now. When he learned from published records on the internet the date of the death of Christine's father, Red Stewart, it wasn't too hard to find out the town where he was buried. It was in the Blue Ridge Mountains of Virginia. He knew one of his contacts had a home near the area so he had asked him to check out the local records. The man had said he'd look into it right away so Ron was hoping to hear from him. He entered "Larry Stewart" into his computer. There must have been a hundred or more "Larry Stewarts" in the country. He'd look again tomorrow. He would narrow his search.

The next morning he took his computer to the kitchen table. He missed having his office but when he had moved to the Retirement Village Ron never thought he would be actively involved in another case. He sat and entered all his information into the system. He was a man who made many notes, then reviewed them quietly, trying to see where his thoughts would lead him. He made two lists: one titled "What I know" and the other was "What I need to know."

The first was easy:

A man claiming to be a long lost relative, believed dead, appeared at Christine's.

Man has wife, (very young) and baby daughter.

Man claims he is on his way from Kentucky to new job in Seattle, Washington.

Man has old car that apparently needs repairs.

Ron thought for a moment then added one more item:

Christine wants to believe he is part of her family: says mannerisms and memories appear to be legitimate.

Then Ron started his second list:

Who is Larry?

Who is Jody?

Where and when did they meet?

Where and when did they get married? Are they even married?

Where and when was baby Bella born?

Then Ron went back to his first list to add another item then decided to make a third list titled "Lies"

Christine's parents did not die in Kentucky or West Virginia. They died in the Blue Ridge Mountains of Virginia.

Ron reread the email from his contact, an old acquaintance that had been in the investigation business. This man said he checked out the town and the funeral home who had received a benefit check from an insurance policy.

When Ron had visited Christine, he and Larry had looked at Larry's car. Supposedly Larry had been having work done on it all week but Ron noticed the car had not been washed for some time which made him wonder how so much dirt got on a hood of a car that would have been opened and shut a lot of times with people working on it. It was just a very small thing but one that Ron noticed. He had made a mental note of the license number on the Kentucky license plate so he entered it into his notes.

He reached for his phone and called a friend, Lt. Joe Sisi, who worked for the Crofton Police Department.

"Ron, it's good to hear from you. It's been a while. Tell me you called to be friendly and not that you are working another case," Joe said when he took the call.

"I wouldn't call it a case, just a curiosity. A friend of mine has had some long-lost relatives appear on her doorstep. I would just like to confirm that are who they say they are. Can you possibly check a license plate for me without getting into trouble? It's from Kentucky." Ron gave Joe the make of the car and the plate number. He waited as Joe entered the information into the computer.

"Whoa," Joe said after entering the number. "This license plate and car don't match. Let me see what I can find out. The car may have just been purchased recently and the plates were switched. I'll check it out and call you back."

While Ron waited he started to check his emails. He re-read the one from his friend, Deke, who lived in the Virginia area.

"I checked some local records in the area of the funeral home that buried Red Stewart. Found nothing to indicate the family ever lived here. I'll leave first thing in the morning. If I get nothing concrete I'll check the names of children who entered the child care system. I'll stay in touch. My wife said to say hello and thank you for getting me out of her way for a day. Do you think my retirement is getting to her?"

This waiting is the hardest emotional part of an investigation, Ron thought as he continued to sift through the notes. The phone rang. He saw from the caller I.D. that it was from the Crofton, P.D.

"Hello, Joe," Ron said as he picked up the phone. "Did you find anything?"

"The license plates were issued to a man in Kentucky for a Ford van. He and his wife took a cross-country camping trip through the south on the way to California. When they got there to visit their daughter they discovered that somewhere along the way the plates had been switched. Their car now had Oklahoma plates on it. I'll keep checking and get back to you."

There must be something more I can do while I wait, Ron thought. He reread all his notes. He read about Baby

Bella. *I wonder why I think she might be the key to all of this. What is it that is nagging me so?* There was something about they way the baby clung to him when he picked her up. She settled against him just the way his own grandkids did. Sometimes when men ignore their kids, Ron had noticed that even babies sense it and are not comfortable when held by a man. But Baby Bella had settled into his arms. Larry certainly never seemed to be extra attentive to her. He wasn't mean to her either. Maybe she had a grandfather back in Kentucky who loved her.

Ron continued to sit at his table and study his notes. He decided not to say anything more to Christine until he had some facts. But her safety worried him. He just couldn't feel good about any of this. But he had no real facts to explain his feelings.

Chapter 12

Christine got up early and decided to fix a really nice breakfast for her new family. Maybe not a fancy French breakfast that she made on occasion for George, but something they might enjoy as a family. She wondered how the investigation was going.

George, I know you're watching over me. I'm sorry I haven't been out to talk with you for so long; it seems like years. But I have this little problem I need to get through. And you don't need to worry. Ron has insisted that I keep his phone number on my cell phone speed dial. I have taken to wearing jeans more often. They have a handy pocket I can keep my phone in so it's always available. Mike calls me every day. When I told him he didn't need to do so, he said his dad would come back and haunt him if he didn't. So many people are so very good to me.

Larry, Jody and Bella came into the kitchen and interrupted her thoughts.

"Good morning," she said with a smile as she took Bella and placed her in the highchair. "How is my sweet baby this morning?"

Turning to Larry and Jody, she invited them to sit at the table while she made Western Omelets to go with the sweet pastries she had made the day before.

As they were enjoying the food, the phone rang. Christine answered promptly.

"Christine, I hope I'm not calling too early. It's Betty Coleman. Ray and I haven't seen you for a while and I decided I better check up on you. Are you OK?"

"I'm fine. I have company in from out of town."

"How nice for you. Then I won't keep you. There is a meeting scheduled tonight about our Civil War dinner. Everything is really starting to move and I think it will be really special. Everyone is anxious to see some of your old relics. That reminds me. I told my daughter, JoAnn, about the Cloisonné vase in your attic. She is really into antiques. She said she spotted one that sounds a lot like yours in a little shop on the west side of town. I told her I would mention it to you since you said you had broken one of yours. I hope you have a good visit with your family. We'll stay in touch."

"Well, that was a nice phone call." Christine said as she sat back down at the table. She told them about the plans for the Civil War dinner. "Maybe we can all go together." She started to tell them about the relics of the Civil War she was providing.

"I don't think we can stay that long." Larry said. "In fact, we need to leave right away. I need to get settled in Seattle, get a job and get a home for my family. I've got the car fixed now. We probably should leave no later than tomorrow. Maybe we should go this afternoon."

Christine looked at them. Larry was suddenly very nervous and Jody looked like she might cry. Christine knew she must not let them leave until she had answers. But what could she do? *Help me, George. Help me, Lord, she thought.*

"Please don't go until we have a chance to say a proper goodbye," she said. Then she reached for her cell phone. She hit the speed-dial number for Ron. Trying to appear calm she sat back down at the table and asked Jody to pour them all more coffee.

"This is Ron," he said, as he answered his phone. "Are you OK Christine?"

"Good morning, Janet," Christine said very smoothly. "Is Mike in today?"

Ron paused for just a moment than answered, "Are you OK? Are you sending me a message? Is the family there with you?"

"Yes, Janet. It's good to talk to you too. But I really need to talk to Mike."

Christine paused for just a moment and heard Ron answer. "I got it Christine. You want them to think you are trying to reach Mike. Go ahead."

"I'm sorry Mike is out of town. Did you say he's on a cruise? When will he be back? Well, I need his help, Janet. I don't know if you know or not but my brother I thought had died childless had a son. The family is visiting with me now. It has been wonderful to have a family in the house. But they are insisting that they need to get on their way again. In fact they may even want to leave later today. I have asked them to stay for a while longer. It has occurred to me that George left me very comfortable financially.

I have no children. I've had a couple of thoughts. One thought is to give them a check to help them on their way and get settled. But I have no way of knowing about the cost of things in Seattle. I want to set up a couple of trust funds; one for my nephew and his wife and one for their baby, my sweet little niece. I'd like it set up so that they get a generous annual income from it. Or maybe I will just transfer a sizable amount of cash to Seattle so they can buy a house. I don't know which is best and I want to talk to Mike about it. I want to be sure there is no problem with them getting the money. I don't want them to wait for me to die to have some financial help."

"Christine, you want me to know they are planning to leave right away? Is that right?" Ron asked.

"Yes, indeed," she said. "We were just sitting here having breakfast when Larry said he thought they should leave right away. I'd like them to stay for a while longer," she said.

"Okay," Ron said. "I'll pretend I'm Janet. Because of money laundering laws it is not so easy to transfer funds. It will take a few days. Trust funds also take time to establish. Tell Larry it will be very easy to do if he is still in town to sign the papers. Tell him Janet will get in touch with Mike and start the paper work. That will stall him for a few more days and give us a chance to get the DNA tests back. I may have them as early as today. I'll phone Mike to make sure Janet doesn't put through the wrong calls to Mike."

"Thank you, Janet. I'll expect your call this afternoon. I do hope you'll be able to reach Mike. I'd hate to have my family leave town before we get things settled."

Christine put her phone back in her pocket, looked at Larry who had a most confused look on his face.

"I'm sure you must have heard my conversation with Mike's secretary. I had this all in mind but it takes time to get things set up. Do you think you might delay your trip for just a few more days? Janet is going to try to reach Mike so she can get the paperwork started. I know it will make things a lot easier for you if you don't have to worry about the money."

"Aunt Tina, I don't know what to say." Larry seemed to stumble over his words. "We can't take any money from you. It wouldn't be right. You need that money to live on."

Christine looked at him carefully. She couldn't tell for sure if he was sincere or planning his next step. And right now, she didn't know what the next step might be. *But if he is my real nephew, I do want to help him with the money,* she thought.

"Tell me you can stay for at least a couple of more days. With the money laundering laws, it's not easy to transfer funds from one bank to another. I do need a couple of days to get it set up. And you'll need a bank account in Seattle to receive the funds. I want to be able to make your move to Seattle a bit smoother. What do I need to do to get you to change your mind?"

"I just feel we've imposed on you too much already. You're being very generous. If it makes it easier for you if we stay a couple more days, I guess we can do it. But at least tell me something I can do to help you while I'm here," Larry said very sincerely.

"Well, maybe there is something you can do. I need to have some items from the attic brought downstairs so I can sort through them to decide what I can offer for the Civil War dinner."

"I'll be glad to do that." Larry seemed deep in thought for a moment or so. "I've been thinking about something. I haven't seen much of this area since we've been here. Are we far from the ocean? I'd love to take a ride through the area. Who knows? This might be a better place to settle than the Seattle area," Larry said with a smile.

"That's a great idea. After we visit the coast we can stop for lunch at a very nice little café that's almost on the water. Let me call Mike's office and let him know I'll be away for most of the day so Janet can leave a message." She reached for her cell phone and hit the speed dial for Ron.

"Hello, Janet, this is Christine again. I just want you to know that my nephew has agreed to stay for at least a couple of more days. We're going to take a drive to the ocean today. If you get any information from Mike, please leave a message on the answering machine."

Ron listened to Christine. "I don't know how you do it, Christine, but you are brilliant. Be careful and stay in touch as often as you can about where you are."

Chapter 13

Ron pressed the end button on his phone and sat with his head in his hand. He wished this investigation was over. He was worried about Christine spending the day away from home at a place where no help was near. His gut feeling, based on many years of investigations, was that there would be more trouble ahead before the case was closed. Will Christine be in danger going so far from home with Larry? Will Larry try to harm Christine with Jody and Bella in the car? Was Christine's offering of money to Larry enough for Larry to want to keep her alive?

I better bring Mike up to date about Christine's phone call, he thought. He called Mike on Mike's private line.

"Christine never fails to amaze me at how quickly she adapts to any situation. I, too, am beginning to worry about her safety. Have you been able to find out any information about the family?" Mike asked.

"My investigation is taking me down many roads. I found out that her father died and is buried in the Blue Ridge Mountains of Virginia. Death benefits were paid to a funeral home in a small town. An investigator will be there this morning to get more information. I'm sure I'll hear more before the end of the day."

Ron continued, "I got DNA samples from Christine and Larry and may hear as early as tonight if they are a match. I'm not sure why but I felt it necessary to get a DNA swab from the baby, too." Ron's voice was full of concern. "But there is something odd about Larry's car," Ron continued. "I asked Joe Sisi – he's a lieutenant at the Crofton P.D. – to run the license plate number and he's uncovered a mystery. He's doing more checking right now and said he'd stop by in about half an hour. Do you know Joe?"

"Yes, I know Joe. I've found him to be a smart, professional young officer. What did he find out?"

"That the plates don't match the car. The plates were stolen from a car somewhere in the southern part of the country while the family was on a trip out west. The owner didn't discover the switch until they were in California. Joe is trying to get more info before he comes over. I guess I'll have to be open with him about this investigation. What do you think?"

Mike thought for a minute. "Yes, I agree. If it's OK with you I'd like to be there when he comes."

"I think that's a good idea. I'll start a pot of coffee."

Mike and Ron were looking over Ron's notes when the doorbell rang. It was Joe who apologized for taking so long to get there.

"It seems we have three cars involved in a license plate switch involving cars from Kentucky, Oklahoma, and Nevada. That tells me this was not a random act, but one carefully planned out. I made some quick phone calls to California and Oklahoma. The only thing that ties them together is that the two out-of-state cars were in Las Vegas at the same time. The family from Kentucky was on its way to California. The family who owned the car with Oklahoma license plate was vacationing in Vegas. The car from Kentucky ended up with Oklahoma plates. The car from Oklahoma ended up with plates from Nevada. And apparently Larry's car in Nevada ended up with plates from Kentucky. This pretty much tells us that the switch was made in Vegas," Joe told them. "But I need information from you. What's going on around here? Stolen plates make this a police matter."

Mike spoke first. "It concerns Christine McCall. Do you know her background?"

"No, I don't know much about her other than she was married to George who was well known and apparently had no money problems. What does that have to do with stolen license plates?"

Mike began to talk. "Christine grew up in West Virginia. She married a local boy when she was seventeen and left home for Nashville. The marriage failed. Christine returned home to learn that her father, mother and young brother named Larry had apparently left home to move to Nashville to be with her. Rumors were that the family had been killed in a car accident. She was unable to confirm it. Eventually she moved to Vegas, married for the second time. Apparently there is some sort of story there but I don't know it. Later she met and married George. George was my father's best friend. When George died, my father took the responsibility for managing Christine's financial affairs. When my dad died, I took over. George's estate has grown considerably since Christine spends very little money." Mike paused and looked at Ron. "Why don't you continue?"

"A couple of Sundays ago Christine came home from church to find a car with Kentucky plates in her driveway. On her porch sat a young man, his wife and baby. He told Christine he was her nephew, the son of her younger brother. She thought the brother was dead all these years."

"Did she do any checking on him?" Joe asked.

"Not at first. He said all the right things, seemed to know about her childhood, and even seemed to have some familiar mannerisms. She let him move into her home. Supposedly he only stopped because his car broke down as he and his family traveled from Kentucky to Seattle where he says he has a job. Christine and I became friends when I asked for her help out at the VA Nursing home. Christine is a shrewd woman. When she told me about Larry I offered to do a background check on him."

Mike then continued, "Like I said, Christine is definitely not hard up for money. And as an estate lawyer, I am always leery of poor relatives who show up on a rich widow's doorstep. Ron and I got together with Christine and decided to do a bit of investigating."

"What have you uncovered so far?" Joe asked.

Ron told him about the information on the death of Christine's family and the fact that he already had DNA samples being processed. He told Joe he was waiting to hear those results. He was also waiting for results of the search in Virginia already underway about the death of her parents and brother.

"Do you think that Christine is in any danger?" Joe asked Ron and Mike.

"We're both very anxious but Christine has been handling it well," Mike said. He then told Joe about the phone calls earlier that morning. "Christine is determined to keep Larry in town until she finds out for sure if he is her nephew."

"I'll have to meet this lady," Joe said. "Shall I have a patrol car go by her house regularly?"

"Let's wait until tonight to decide. I'm expecting word about the burial of her family and also the DNA tests."

"How did you get him to agree to a DNA test?" Joe asked.

"I told Christine to invite me for dinner. I brought some beer which we drank while we cooked steaks…"

"And you got the sample from the bottle. Good thinking, Ron. That will save a lot of time. Do we have Christine's DNA on file?"

Ron gave a small grin. "I had no way of knowing so I did a swab on her also. And I did one on the baby. Somehow I think the baby is involved in this. That little family doesn't seem quite right to me."

Ron's cell phone rang.

"Hello Ron. This is Deke, calling from a little town in Virginia and I have hit a jackpot of information for you. So much I decided to call you as I sit here in the kitchen of a very nice lady who helped to bury Christine's parents and brother."

"Wonderful, Tell me everything," Ron said. He quickly told Mike and Joe who was calling and put the call on the speaker.

"I'm with Martha Collins, who many years ago started her career working in the office of a local funeral home. Very early one morning a call came from the state police asking them to transport three bodies to the home from an accident site in the mountains. From items removed from the car they learned the names of the occupants, a family named Stewart, all of whom had died. When they called the home town to get burial instructions they were informed there was no family left in the home town. There was no one to take responsibility for the burial. The police found a box full of family business papers, insurance policies, pictures, and a letter written to a Christine Parker in Nashville that had been returned by the Post Office marked undeliverable. The town decided to give the family a decent burial. They purchased three lots in the local cemetery. The family had some insurance money which was used to help pay for the lot and burial expenses." Deke paused and then continued.

"Martha Collins was very sad about the events that had taken the lives of this family. She carefully read every paper in the box and determined that Christine was a daughter who had left home. Martha felt she had to take care of each and every item they were able to retrieve from the car as well as the newspaper accounts and police reports of the accident. She said she knew that someday the daughter would come looking for information and she wanted to keep it for her. Martha has since retired from the funeral home but she took the box with her and kept it in her attic. I now have possession of that box. Do you want me to ship it to you overnight express when I get back to the city or do you want me to go through it for more information first?"

"Why don't you take it for overnight shipping? I'll call you back within the hour if I think of anything else. Be sure to include Martha's name and address and maybe the names of anyone else who might have helped in the burial. I know Christine will want to contact them."

"Is this the information you needed to close your case?" Deke asked Ron.

"I certainly could not close this case without it, but I'm afraid it has opened more paths to travel. We have been told the parents were buried in Kentucky or Tennessee and the son grew up in the foster system. I'm not sure why we were given this information. But thanks so much for your help. I'll keep you posted on what I find."

"Glad to help. If there is anything else, please call me. I'll be anxious to hear about all of it."

Mike and Joe had been listening as Ron had talked.

"Another loose end to tie up," Ron told them.

"I've just had a thought," Joe said. "One bit of information we don't have are the names of the owners of the cars that had the license plates switched. That might help in the investigation. I'll head back to the station and do some research."

Mike looked at Ron and said, "Now we know that Larry has been lying. I'm even more worried about Christine. I wonder who Larry really is."

"And I have a new worry," Ron said. "How and when do I tell Christine about this new information?"

They sat quietly for a few minutes, each one deep in thought. "I think I want to check on Christine," Mike said. He reached for his phone and entered her number. She answered almost immediately.

"Christine, it's Mike," he said in his most lawyerly voice in case Christine had her speaker turned on. "My secretary just called me here on the cruise ship. I hear you may want to set up a couple of trust funds. I think it's a great way for you to provide for your nephew and his family. I want to draw it up myself instead of having my staff do it. I'm going to leave the ship as soon as we reach a port and fly back home. I'll get right on it."

"That sounds wonderful, Mike. Can you wait a moment please?" Mike heard her asking Larry if they could stay a few more days and that Mike was going to hurry home. "Larry says they'll stay through the weekend."

"If you are sure that *you're okay* right now with these plans, tell me you really appreciate me. If you're not... I'll try to make other..."

Christine understood his conversation; that he was concerned for her, and interrupted him. "I do so appreciate you, Mike. I'm sorry I interrupted your vacation. You are a very good man. We are having a very nice visit but my nephew is anxious to get settled in Seattle."

As Mike hung up he turned to Ron and said, "I knew I was getting a lot of gray hair but I bet I'll be white-haired before we're done with this. I should get back to the office for a bit. I need to talk with Janet so she will not let anyone know my movements. She's very curious about what is happening. She usually knows everything I do."

After Mike left, Ron made more notes and added information into his computer. He started to feel he was beginning to get control of this situation. If he just had at least part of the DNA information, he'd be more comfortable about what to do next. He reached for his cell phone and called the lab.

"Sorry if I'm rushing you but do you have any news for me," he asked.

"I have the results on the first two samples you gave me. The two people from whom you took the samples are not related. I won't know if the baby is a relative for another day or so," the lab manager told him.

Ron sat back quietly in his chair. In all his years of corporate investigations, the trails took him through what someone had done. His job was to find out who was the person that did it. This was different. Now he had to figure out who the people really were.

The phone rang.

"Hi, it's Joe. I came back to a problem that takes a top priority. I'll check on who owned the license plates as soon as I can and call you. If you want us to start to patrol near Christine's house or want us to watch for her car between here and the coast, let me know."

Ron sat quietly at his kitchen table with his head in his hand. He decided to reread all his notes again. He read the notes he had made from his conversation with Deke. He was anxious to get the box from Virginia and sift through it. A feeling of gloom came over him. He felt he was missing something he should be finding. He worried about how and when to tell Christine. He felt she should not be spending another night in a house with strangers who might do her harm. What excuse could he use to get her out of the house? He had a feeling she wouldn't want to leave but he'd have to try something. He decided to call Mike, update him on the news that Larry and Christine were not relatives, and ask him for ideas.

"Hi, Mike. Christine and Larry are not blood relatives."

"I knew it. I just knew it. We have to get Christine out of the house."

"I agree. Any ideas on how we do it?"

"Maybe I could call her 'from the ship' and ask her to baby-sit with my kids overnight. I can tell her that the nanny got sick or something."

"That might work. I'm still waiting for the report on the license plates. Joe said he had a top priority job to do first. Mike, what do you think is really going on here? If it's all money related, someone had to do a lot of research to carry it this far. It must be someone from her past. But who could that be?"

"Apparently someone who knew her as a child," Mike answered. "Maybe a cousin or someone."

"I got another call coming in. I'll keep you posted," Ron said as he pushed the end and receive button on his phone. He checked the caller ID.

"Hello, Joe."

"Ron, got your pen handy? I got the names and addresses of the car owners. The one I think we should start with is the car owner from Vegas. The plates were issued to a Jane Parker. Except for a speeding ticket and unpaid parking tickets there is no file on her. She is a woman about twenty-five years old, married to a man named Donald. She has a job as a waitress. Her husband is apparently on some sort of disability. There is a short police jacket on Donald, mostly petty crimes: loitering, harassment of people on the streets, and so on. I asked the Vegas P.D. to fax over his picture. They said they'd do it right away. Do you want me to drop it off on my way home tonight or wait till tomorrow?"

"Joe, I'd like to see it as soon as I can. I got the DNA results back for Larry and Christine and they are not related. Something is up. I'm feeling very uneasy."

Joe was silent for a moment. "Ron, I think it's time I bring the chief up-to-date. I recommend we set up a headquarters here where we will have access to police files. Bring your information and come on over. Let's ask Mike to join us. As her attorney he needs to represent Christine. Will you call him or should I?"

Ron said he'd phone Mike.

Chapter 14

Christine did a lot of thinking as she drove to the coast. She knew from the tone in Mike's voice that he was concerned about her. She did feel a bit more comfortable knowing that Mike and Ron were helping her. As she walked along the shore of the Pacific she did wish she had just a bit of time alone to walk to the rock and talk to George but she knew it would not be a good idea to mention it.

She led them down the path to the place where the otters were playing. Jody was so excited to see them.

"Did you know that otters are the only mammals to use tools?" Jody asked. "They use rocks to break open shells or to break away debris around their food. They're very buoyant and wrap themselves in kelp to keep warm and dry in the winter."

"You must have studied a lot about them," Christine said.

"Oh, I did. I just love them. I never had a chance to see a real one before," she answered.

It was only the second time Christine had seen Jody enthused about anything, the first being when she got her new jeans. As they walked to the restaurant, Jody asked Larry if she might have a few minutes to sit by the water. He told her yes but he would be watching her.

Christine overheard the exchange of words. *That's odd. What made him say that? I'll have to remember to tell Ron and Mike about it.*

As they ate lunch Christine decided to probe a bit. "We've been together for a couple of weeks now. I'd like to know more about you both. Tell me about your family, Jody. Where did you grow up? Do you have any sisters or brothers? How did you and Larry meet?"

Larry answered for her. "She's a Kentucky kid. She has an older brother who was a friend of mine."

Jody kept her eyes down on her plate, and then only looked at the baby.

Well, that didn't work. I'll try a different way, Christine thought.

"You must have been very young when you gave birth to Bella. I bet your parents were thrilled to have such a beautiful grandchild."

Larry answered, "They weren't happy. That's another reason we left Kentucky. We can get a new start on our own." He paused and then continued, "You know something, Aunt Tina," I don't feel right taking any money from you even though it certainly would make it a lot easier for us to have a little help."

Larry never took his eyes off Jody.

"That's what relatives are for," Christine said. "Families should always be there for each other. My attorney has been very careful about investments of the money George left me. I'll be glad to help you when you leave here. I want you to be able to use the money without any interference. If you're careful you might never need to work again. I'll try to make sure it is set up that way."

"You are a very kind woman. My dad always said you were. Thank you, Aunt Tina."

In spite of his words he seemed to be nervous and jumpy in ways he had not been before. *Something has set him off. But what can it be? He's much too slick and sweet to me. I do believe he's up to something. I'll be glad when this is over. Or should I just end this now? I'll talk to Ron and Mike as soon as we get back home,* Christine decided.

Jody turned to Larry. "Can I go sit on the beach for just few more minutes?"

"No, he answered. "We've already taken too much of Aunt Tina's time. We need to get back on the road."

"Nonsense," Christine told him as she turned to Jody. "You just go and sit there and enjoy the beautiful scenery. We have all the time we want to enjoy being together."

Larry spoke sternly. "No, we should get right back. I appreciate what you want to do for us, Aunt Tina. You probably think that's all I ever wanted. You're wrong. I wanted a family. I think we should leave right away. We can stay in touch. If you want to remember us in your will that would be nice but we need to leave."

Jody surprised Christine by speaking up. "Can I have at least ten minutes by the water or maybe just five minutes?" she asked Larry.

"No. We need to be on our way," he said sharply.

Christine spoke up. "Of course you can have your ten minutes. I'll sit with you. Don't worry, Larry. I'll drive fast to get home and make up the time." Christine gently pulled Jody along with her as she spoke the words.

As they approached the water Christine put her arm around Jody. She saw the tears start to flow from Jody's eyes. Christine said nothing. They sat by the water silently.

"How old are you?" she asked Jody.

Jody said nothing.

"Did Larry tell you not to talk to me?"

"Yes."

"Are you afraid of him?"

"Yes."

"Can you tell me why?"

"He'll kill me and the baby."

Christine felt ice water flowing through her body.

"Did he say those words?"

"Yes."

"Hey, it's time for us to leave," Larry called as he walked toward them. He looked at Jody and saw her tear-stained cheeks.

"I thought I told you to stop your whining. Come on. We've got to leave here. We have to leave for Seattle tonight."

Christine spoke quietly. "Larry, I think Jody's feeling a little homesick. We'll leave right away for home. Please, out of respect for me, be kind to her. I know what it's like to be separated from your family."

They slowly made their way to the car. Christine knew she must find a way to delay their departure to Seattle.

"I need to let Betty Coleman know I will not be attending the planning meeting for the Civil War dinner tonight. I'll make a quick call right now." Christine reached for her cell phone and hit the speed dial for Ron.

"Hello, Betty. This is Christine. Can you talk for a minute? I'm currently on my way back to Crofton from the coast. My nephew and his wife are going to be leaving tonight so I won't be at your meeting." She paused to give Ron a chance to understand her message. Then she thought of something. "Oh, by the way, Betty, do you remember that picture of the young girl and child that I gave you to get appraised? Don't bother. I looked it up on the internet and found out it is a phony. The artist whose name is on the picture did not paint it. It is a fraud. I'll tell you all about it tomorrow."

She heard Ron sound puzzled for just a second or so and then he said. "Are you telling me that Jody might be someone else? Do you think Larry may be holding her hostage? Do you believe her?"

"Yes. I know we are both very disappointed to find that it's a fake."

"Do you know who she is?" Ron asked.

"No."

"Did he threaten her?"

"Yes."

"To kill her?"

"Yes."

"Do you feel safe enough to drive home? What route will you be coming home?"

"Yes, Betty. We've had a very nice day. We're getting ready to get on to Pikesville Road. I'll call you later." Christine saw that Larry was becoming very agitated by the delay in their departure.

She put her phone back in her pocket and tried to concentrate on her driving. She had no idea what she would do once they reached home. *Would they even make it home?*

Chapter 15

R on pushed the gas pedal a little harder as he hurried to the police station. From the car seat he picked up his laptop computer with the information he had compiled and hurried into the building.

Joe Sisi was waiting for him with another officer. He handed Ron a picture that had just come in of a man named Donald Parker, the man whom they thought might be involved in the switching of the license plates.

Ron took one look at it and said, "That's the man I met calling himself Larry Stewart. There's something about the name of Parker. Let me check my notes. But I do have some news from Christine. She's on her way home. Larry says he's leaving tonight. Christine got Jody to talk a little. Jody told her that Larry said he would kill both her and the baby if she talks to anyone." He told Joe about the conversation with Christine. While they were talking, Mike joined them.

"I'll call the Sheriff's department right away and ask them to keep track of her car," Joe said as he reached for the phone. "We'll have to plan carefully. If Larry gets desperate he might get very dangerous. I wonder what set him off. He is acting like a man who has been spooked. I had hoped we could keep him in town until we get something to hold him on. Do you know if he carries a gun?"

"I don't know."

While they were talking two more police officers, Ralph and Ed came into the room. "The chief briefed us and told us to report for duty," they told Joe.

Joe took charge. "Our number one goal is the safety of Christine and the baby. Next is the safety of the girl. She may or may not be a part of the scam. Larry might be holding her as hostage. Based on what I've been told I don't believe the girl will say anything in front of Larry. We know he's not who he says he is but we don't know for sure who he is. We do know he has information about Christine's past. We know he's up to no good. We need a plan to separate them quickly as soon as they arrive back in town. Ralph, I've got the Sheriff's Department tailing her from the coast on Pikesville Road. Get a patrol car in place to tail the car as soon as it crosses into the city limits. I think we need to make it a very soft take-down without lights and sirens if we can. It might spook him into taking chances."

"How about waiting for them to arrive back home," Ed said. "Let's have a couple of cars on-scene and tell Christine and Larry there was a report of a break-in in the neighborhood. We'll ask the family to wait outside while supposedly Christine goes through the house with another officer to see if anything is missing. Christine could be taken to safety."

Ralph spoke up. "You said there is a problem with the license plates. Let's mention it to Larry We'll play it low-key and then ask Larry to go to the station with us just to get the problem cleared up."

"What about the girl and the baby?" Ron asked. "We can't let anything happen to the baby."

They seemed a bit stumped as they sat there.

Ron had continued to look through his notes as he talked. "I think I've found something. I knew the name Parker rang a bell. There is a box of business and personal papers on its way to me that contains information on the death of the real Larry Stewart. There is an envelope that was mailed and then returned to the family as non-deliverable. The woman who kept the box said it was to someone named Christine Parker. She decided it was a family member. Parker may be the name of Christine's first husband. There may be a connection."

"It's another lead for us to follow. It makes sense. Her ex would have known family history. Maybe Larry is the son of that man. But we can't think about that now," Joe said. "We must get Christine to safety.

A young woman came into the room. "I'm Sgt. Diana Atlantis. The chief said you might need my help."

They gave her a quick update and told her they needed a way to gently get the young girl and baby safely to the police station. They needed something legal, yet didn't want to scare Jody. They needed time to check things out.

"I've brought in quite a few young teen-age girls for shoplifting. Could we use that?" Diane asked.

"It's too weak," Joe said.

"Maybe not," Ron answered. "Christine bought her a new outfit. I bet she has it on today. Let's say it matches something that was lifted at the store and ask her to produce a receipt. It might buy us a little time."

Joe's cell phone rang. He took the call and told them, "Christine's car has just arrived in Crofton. We need to move fast. I want everyone in place in Christine's drive way before she pulls in. Remember, no lights or sirens. Ralph, take over the license plate query and bring Larry in. Diana, you question the girl about shop-lifting. I'll take Christine. That leaves the baby."

"Both Christine and Jody will want to keep the baby," Ron told them.

"We'll see how that goes. Take back-up with you," Joe told the officers. "Brief them on the plan. Remember, no lights or sirens. We want them to be surprised when they see police cars in the driveway. We have less than ten minutes so let's get everyone in place."

One of the officers asked, "Is he packing a gun?"

Joe looked at Ron and Mike.

"We have no idea," they told him.

"Well, stay alert. Let's go," Joe told his crew. Turning to Mike and Ron he said, "You can ride with me. But stay in the patrol car until both Larry and Jody are under our control."

Chapter 16

Christine tried to drive very carefully on the way back to Crofton. She was certain that Ron and Mike were planning to help her but how can they plan something this quickly? She noticed a car behind her that seemed to keeping the same pace as she was. She wondered if she was being tailed. She tried from time to time to make small talk but got only a yes or no as a response back from Larry. She got nothing from Jody.

"Shall we stop at a drive-thru and pick up sandwiches to eat tonight," Christine suggested.

"No, I'm anxious to get on the road."

"Why not wait and give me one more night with my precious family," Christine suggested.

"No, we have to hit the road. Jody, you have ten minutes to pack our things."

As they pulled into Christine's neighborhood, they saw two police cars blocking the street. Christine stopped. "Is there something wrong, officer?" she asked.

"Nothing for you to worry about, ma'am. We've had a report of several break-ins in the area so we're trying to check each house and anyone who comes in or out. May I see your driver's license, please?"

Christine showed him her license and he waved her through to her street. She saw three police cars in front of her house.

"Well, this is a first," Christine said. "I wonder what's going on."

Joe Sisi approached her. "Are you Christine McCall? Please step out of the car and show me your I.D. The two of you remain in the car," he commanded Jody and Larry. Another police officer stood nearby watching the car.

"I want you to go with me into your house to see if anything is disturbed or missing," Christine was told. She took her house key from her purse and unlocked the door. Christine started to feel very nervous. *A possible break-in at my home on the end of this nerve-wracking day I've already had,* she thought. She wasn't sure she could make it in the door.

Joe closed the door quickly behind her.

"Sorry, if I shook you up, ma'am, but it was the quickest plan we could come up with to get you to safety. Your home appears perfectly safe. We'll give you a full accounting as soon as possible."

Her cell phone rang.

"It's Ron, Christine. Mike and I are out in the car. We'll be in as soon as we can and explain everything to you. We think we know what's going on. Does the name Parker mean anything to you?"

"Roger Parker was the name of my first husband. Is he behind this? I don't think he'd do this."

"We'll explain everything as soon as we can," he told her.

"Larry has threatened to kill the baby if Jody talks. Can you get the baby to me?" Christine asked Joe. "Bella shouldn't be held responsible for the evil deeds of her father."

"I'll have to see how this plays out. The police are putting Larry into the patrol car. Mike and Ron will be here in just a couple more minutes," Joe told her.

Christine looked out the window. In the early evening dusk she could see that Larry had been handcuffed and was being put into a police car. She saw a female police office talking with Jody.

"I'm not sure what is going on," Christine told Joe Sisi, "but this afternoon Jody told me that Larry said he would kill her and the baby if she didn't do as he told her. I think it explains why she never talked openly. Just a few yeses or nos. She really has tried to be a good mother to Bella. And she's very, very young. Please try to give her the benefit of your doubts. I believe she is a young woman who got caught up in something very bad."

"We'll certainly try ma'am. Here comes Ron and Mike. I'll let them bring you up to date on everything while we start to sort this out."

"Can Jody and the baby stay here with me?"

"At this time I want to take Jody to the station to see if she can tell us anything. Are you comfortable taking care of the baby for a while? I need to head back to the station."

"Of course I will. Will Jody be coming back home tonight."

"Probably, if I feel she's had no part in this. Your safety and the baby's safety come first."

Joe went to the car and talked with the officer who brought the baby to Christine.

Ron and Mike came into the house as the two police cars left, one with Larry and one with Jody.

"Are you okay, Christine?" Ron asked her.

"Well, I think I'm okay. Joe asked me to keep Bella with me. But I'm terribly confused. Did you find out who Larry is? And why did you ask about Roger Parker? I'm very worried about Jody and the baby. Why can't Jody stay here with me?" Christine asked as she began to tend to the baby.

"Mike why don't you bring Christine up-to-date while I make some coffee?" Ron asked.

Mike paused. His face was sad. "Christine, there is no easy way to say this. Ron has confirmed that your parents and brother died in an auto accident in Virginia."

"If my brother died then Larry is not my nephew. How does he know about…? Wait a minute. Larry said the accident was in Kentucky or West Virginia."

"We have confirmed where all three members of your family are buried. For some reason they traveled the Virginia route to get to Nashville."

"I know why they did that," Christine said. "My dad always promised to take my mother back to where she grew up: the Blue Ridge Mountains of Virginia. They never had enough money to make the trip. Dad probably chose to go that way to please my mother. Are you sure they're dead?"

Ron spoke. "My friend Deke has sent me a box which should be here very soon. It contains personal and business papers that were in the car. When the police in Virginia contacted your hometown to ask about burial arrangements, no one there could give the police any information. The residents of the little town in Virginia buried your family. A lady who worked at the funeral home detailed everything. She saved the box all these years because she found a record of you and was sure that someday you would come looking for it."

"But I never did that," Christine said softly as she began to weep.

Mike went to her, to hold her and let her cry. Ron brought coffee. They sat there quietly, giving Christine time to compose herself.

"I'm so confused," she finally said. "How does Larry fit into this? Or I guess I should ask who Larry is? Why did he do this to me?"

Ron began to talk. "Those are answers we don't have yet. But through DNA we did confirm that you and Larry are not related. The car he was driving is registered to a June Parker who is married to a Donald Parker. Donald Parker has been in a bit of trouble with the law, nothing very serious, but during the bookings, the police took his picture. Here is a picture of him."

"That's Larry," Christine said in a shocked voice as she looked at the police shot. "Who is he and what is he trying to do?"

"We're still gathering that information. We suspect he might have been after your money. Something must have spooked him this morning for him to change his plans to try to leave so quickly. Can you think of anything that happened?"

"Not really. I thought about having your number on speed dial so I phoned you, Ron. I wanted you to know where I would be today in case I turned up missing. But I decided to pretend I was talking to you, Mike. He knew you managed my money. I hoped that if he thought he was going to get some money he might stay around longer. We needed time to check him out. He seemed very contrite when he heard about the money and even offered to help me around the house."

"Did you tell him he could do anything?" Mike asked.

"I don't think so. Well, I did ask him to help me bring some relics downstairs from the attic. I'm going to use them for the Civil War Dinner."

Ron spoke up. "Maybe he's been helping himself to those things and didn't want you to know. Do you have lights up there? Could we go up now?

"Of course," Christine said. She laid the baby on a blanket on the floor and led him up to the third floor of the house. She gave a quick look around and began to shake. "All those precious relics are gone. He must have sold all of them. He said he was getting day jobs and seemed to have about $80-$100 each day. Betty Coleman and I were just up here a few days before they came." She paused for a few seconds. "Oh, no, now I remember something. I had a big Cloisonné vase. It isn't here. It was one of a pair but I had broken one. This morning Betty told me her daughter had seen one just like it on the west side of town at an antique shop. I told Larry about it. He must have been afraid I'd go up there looking for the vase."

"I'm sure the police will want an inventory tomorrow to try to locate the articles," Mike said. "I wonder how everything is going at the station. Do you think Larry will talk to Joe?"

"Who knows? I'm wondering about Jody. I bet she's so afraid right now," Christine told them.

I think it's time for me to go to the station," Mike said. "I feel certain Jody is a juvenile and should have legal representation."

"Please take care of her. I really don't think Jody is part of this plot. For the first time she opened up to me a little. First it was about the otters we saw. She was very intelligent about them. Then she sat alone and looked out on the water and seemed miles away. A little later when we were ready to leave she asked Larry for just five or ten minutes longer to sit there. He got extremely nasty with her. I pretended to fluff it off but I quietly asked her if she was afraid of Larry and she said yes. That's when she told me about his threat. Larry was extremely agitated and wanted to get home. I told him I would drive fast to get here quickly. For some reason I felt I was being followed. Did you arrange that?"

"Joe arranged that," Mike told her. "We had to really scramble for a way to separate you, Jody and the baby from Larry."

"Well, apparently it worked very well. I couldn't figure out what was happening. It was all so fast," Christine said.

Ron's cell phone rang. He took the call from Joe Sisi and then told them that Larry was giving the police a lot of trouble. They planned to hold him at least overnight. But Jody wouldn't say a word. They had her in a holding room.

Christine spoke up. "She might talk with me. She opened up a little while we were on the beach. Ask Joe if I can talk to her."

"Joe said he might need you to do so tomorrow. They just need a bit more information tonight and I think they'll let her go."

Are you afraid to have her in the house?" Mike asked.

'No, I'm not afraid."

"Then I'll head to the station and bring her back here if they'll let me. One more thing: Joe asked that you not go into the bedroom Larry slept in until they make a search of it tomorrow. Is that a problem?" Mike asked.

"Well, Bella's bed is there and I need some diapers from the room."

"I'll get what you need. If it's okay with you, Christine, I think we will all feel more comfortable if I spend the night on the couch. Do you mind?" Ron asked.

"Of course I don't mind," she told him. "I'd feel much safer."

Ron went upstairs to move the crib into Christine's bedroom while she finished feeding the baby and got her ready for the night. Little Bella was oblivious to all of them as she settled into her crib.

"Ron, do you mind telling me again what happened today and tonight. I feel like my head is reeling."

Ron told her about the events of the day: getting the DNA reports that showed Larry and Christine were not related, learning about the actual death and burial of her parents and brother and the switch of the license plates. Then he continued, "When I saw the picture of Donald Parker, who was apparently involved in the license plate switching, I recognized him immediately. We set up a headquarters down at the police station so we had the full resources available. When I got your call about the scam we were all very, very concerned for your safety. With a minimum of direction and planning Joe requested that the county sheriff arrange for someone to follow you to the city limits where the Crofton P.D. was waiting. Everyone cooperated and the apprehension went smoothly."

"Do you know if he is Roger's son?"

"Not for sure. The investigation is still going on."

"I just can't believe Roger planned all these details. He was only interested in becoming a star when I last saw him. But that was forty years ago." She shook her head as she talked. They heard the closing of a car door and Jody came into the house.

"Oh Aunt Tina, can you tell me what's going on? The police said I stole these clothes. I told them you bought them for me but they didn't believe me. Is Larry here? He's going to be so mad at me. Please don't leave me alone with him. I'm afraid he will hurt the baby. Where is the baby? Is she okay?"

Christine gave her a hug and gently led her upstairs so that she could see Bella safely sleeping in Christine's room. "I'm going to let you sleep in this room in my bed tonight. You will be safe here. Larry will not be here tonight. Why don't you take a hot shower and get into these clean PJ's and come back downstairs. I'm going to fix a sandwich for you and then we'll talk."

Christine closed the door and went downstairs. Ron was on the phone again. When he ended the call he told Christine that because the license plates were not legal on the car they had enough to hold Larry overnight. They expected to have additional charges by morning. He also told her that Christine should expect a full search of the house by the police the next morning. The police were trying to confirm a few facts before confronting Larry with the picture of Donald Parker.

Jody came downstairs in her oversized pajamas and wet hair pulled back into a ponytail.

"Is Larry going to be in jail all night? He'll be so mad tomorrow."

"I'm afraid Larry has gotten himself into some trouble. The license plates on his car were not issued for his car. The police are trying to get it figured out," Ron told her.

"Did Aunt Tina tell you where we went today?"

"I believe she said you went to the ocean. Did you have a good time?"

"Almost all of it was wonderful. We saw some otters. I've read a lot about them but this is the first time I ever saw real ones. They are so much fun to watch and they're so smart and …"

Christine's mind drifted as she half-listened to the conversation. Jody was like an animated young girl, not a woman with a child and a husband in jail. But suddenly

Jody stopped talking and again changed into the quiet, scared woman. "I have to go back to jail tomorrow," she told them.

"I think you mean you need to go the police station tomorrow, not go to jail. They simply want to get a formal statement from you. Did you know the license plates were not legal?" Ron asked.

"No."

"Well, we really shouldn't talk about that tonight," Christine said. "If you want to get in bed and read a while I don't think the light will bother Bella."

"It will be so nice to sleep in a bed tonight."

"I don't understand," Christine said. "What do you mean about sleeping in a bed?"

"Larry wanted the bed so I slept on the floor."

"What?" Christine almost shouted.

"I think this conversation should wait till tomorrow," Ron said. "You should get a good night's sleep tonight."

"I am pretty sleepy. I'll do these dishes and then go to bed."

"The dishes can wait," Christine told her. "Let me tuck you in tonight. We'll talk tomorrow." Christine gently led her up the stairs.

When Christine came back downstairs Ron had cleared the table and was taking a phone call.

Christine was in a furry. "Can you believe he made her sleep on the floor?" she asked.

"Yes, I can believe it. I saw the blankets and pillow in the corner when I moved the crib," he told her. "Sit down, Christine; I've just ended a call with Joe. He and

Mike and the crew will be working all night on this case. I also checked my messages while you were upstairs. I had a very important one. The DNA test on Bella has been completed. Larry is not her father."

"Do you think she's Jody's baby?"

"We'll have to wait until Joe or the FBI talks with Jody tomorrow."

"The FBI?"

"State lines were probably crossed. The FBI will be heading up the investigation now. This case has gotten much bigger than someone trying to get money from you."

"I can't believe all this is happening. It seems to go on and on."

"Why don't you try to get some rest tonight? Tomorrow will be a busy, busy day for you."

Christine got some blankets and pillows and put them in the library for Ron to get some rest on the big sofa there. She took a blanket and pillow and tried to rest on the sofa in the living room.

Chapter 17

Christine tossed and turned on the sofa, unable to sleep for more than fifteen minutes at a time. She wanted to get up but was afraid her movements might awaken Ron, Jody or the baby. She relived every word about Larry/ Donald. Is it really true that he is Roger's son? *That's too far-fetched,* she thought. *There has to be some logical explanation.* She couldn't remember even thinking about Roger since the day she told George about it many, many years earlier. Still, it's possible the mannerisms she thought were from her family might have been those of Roger. He was at her house constantly. He had gone with her to the library many times. He listened when she read to her little brother about the little engine. Remembering this led Christine to think about her family. *There're really gone. I guess it's good for me to have this closure. Down deep I always knew they were dead yet a small part of me did so want to believe that they might be alive. But my mother and father loved me. Some way or other they would have found me.*

Christine started to become aware of a smell in the air. Could it be… It was. It was definitely coffee. She made her way to the kitchen. Ron was sitting at the kitchen table once more at his computer poring over the notes he had made.

"Sorry if I woke you. Sit down here. I'll pour you some coffee. Hope you don't mind that I've made myself at home in your kitchen."

"Did you get any sleep?" she asked.

"Very little. I've got a lot of information to include in my notes. If I was a regular working man instead of retired, I'd probably be a lot quicker to figure this out. I thought my working days were over."

They heard a soft knock at the back door. Christine went to open it.

"I must not have wakened you. You came to the door too fast." Mike said. "Is it too early for a cup of coffee?"

"Sit right here. I'll get another cup," Christine told him. "Why are you here so early?'

"I've been at the station all night. I was on my way home to change clothes and decided to come this way. When I saw the light on I took a chance you might be up already."

"Is there anything new to report?" Ron asked.

"Joe kept his whole crew on duty all night. This is probably the biggest case this town has ever seen. He's making sure that every legal step is followed so that he has an airtight case if and when it goes to court."

"I guess Joe told you about Bella's DNA not matching Larry's," Ron said.

"Yes. Now we have the new mystery of who Bella really is," Mike told them.

Christine asked, "Is it possible the baby belongs to Jody?

"Anything is possible. But I don't think so," Mike answered. "But that's just a hunch."

"I would imagine that Joe has already called the Feds," Ron told Mike.

"Yes. He had to do it. Crossing state lines makes this a federal case," Mike told them.

"Does Joe have any ideas about the baby, who she is or where she is from?" Christine asked.

Mike answered, "Not yet, but Joe has been on the phone with the chief of police in Vegas and the Feds are involved. In the meantime, Larry/Donald has clammed up about anything. They need to check a few more facts before they question him about Bella. Christine, I've been wondering about something. Do you have any information about your ex-husband that might help us? Any relatives or good friends or just anything?" Mike asked.

"It's been forty years since I saw him or thought about him. I can remember nothing more than I told you; the reason for our marriage, moving to Nashville and eventually to Vegas. I came home from my job as a waitress one day and caught him in bed with a young girl. I only saw him once after that day. It was the day I told him I was divorcing him." Christine paused and put her head down. "Have you found out anything that ties him to this. It is so sad to think he might be a party to this scam."

"Not at this time. The questions go on."

The three of them sat quietly for a few minutes. Then Christine looked at them and said "You two have been through too many hours without sleep and food. I'm going to fix breakfast." She began to reach into the refrigerator.

The two men looked at each other, shrugged their shoulders and smiled.

"I'll make you a French omelet." She started to brown the sausage and cut up the onions, peppers and mushrooms to add to the eggs she had whisked.

"Maybe you'd better make me two omelets," Mike said with a smile. "Something smells delicious."

As they began to eat they heard sounds on the stairs and knew that Jody was bringing the baby down.

"Were you afraid I'd run away?" Jody asked Mike and Ron.

"No, ma'am," Mike told her. "I heard you give Christine your word that you will cooperate with the police. If Christine trusts you, than I do too. So this is baby Bella," he said. "Hello, you beautiful baby."

The baby responded as she had with Ron, rewarding him with a beautiful smile and lots of baby gibberish. Mike responded back as if she was telling him a big story. Jody began to smile and said to Mike, "I think she likes you."

"Let me feed her," Mike said as he took the bowl of baby food from Jody. "I did this for all four of my kids and now I get to do it for my grandchildren. Open up, Bella, here comes a little airplane into the hanger."

The baby started to laugh and banged her little hands into the bowl of cereal. They all started to laugh and then Jody began to cry. She cried loud and hard. "I tried to be like a mother to her but I didn't know how," she told them. "If her daddy goes to jail who will take care of her?"

"Are you Bella's mother?" Christine asked.

"No, no, no," Jody said.

"What do you know about the baby, Jody?" Ron asked. "Did Larry ever say where she was born or when her birthday was? Did she have any brothers or sisters? Can you remember anything at all he might have said about the baby?"

"Larry didn't tell me anything. I told him I needed to know so I would know what kind of baby food to buy. But he said it didn't matter – to buy anything. I was afraid if I got it for an older baby she might choke on it. So I bought the strained food. I didn't know what to do."

"You did very well, Jody. You have been a good mother to this child," Ron told her. She started to cry again.

"Jody," Christine said quietly. "Do you want to talk with your parents?"

"I don't know," she sobbed. "They might be mad."

Christine turned to Mike. "Is it too soon for her to call home?"

"Let me call Joe." He reached for his phone.

"Joe wants to talk with you first, Jody" Mike said. "A couple of officers will be here soon. They are going to do a thorough search of your house and garage, Christine," he said looking her way. "A tow truck is coming to take Larry's car to the impound lot so they can search it." He turned to Jody. "Joe wants to see you, Jody, at the station at 10:30 this morning. Larry may have done things that are not legal. Joe will ask you many questions. He wants us to bring baby Bella. If you answer all of Joe's questions very honestly, this whole thing may be over very quickly."

"Why do we have to take the baby?" she asked.

"I'm sure Joe has a good reason," Mike said. He turned to Jody, "Once that's over you should be free to call anyone you like." Mike smiled at her and said, "I bet you have a boyfriend back home, don't you?"

Her face got a little flushed. "Well, sort of. My dad said I was too young to date."

"Dads are like that," he said. "We want to keep our little girls beside us as long as we can."

"But my dad told me to leave so I'd be famous," she told him.

Mike looked a bit embarrassed and said, "Well, even the best dads sometimes make mistakes."

Christine said, "I need to shower and change." She looked at Mike and Ron. "Will you be staying for a while?"

As Mike nodded, Ron said, "We'll be here as long as you need us."

Mike played peek-a-boo with Bella while Jody began to clear the table. Ron started to help her.

"I bet you hate me, don't you?" she asked him.

"I really like you. You are very good to Bella. But I think that somehow you got into a big mess of trouble. But as long as you are honest, Christine, Mike and I are here to help you. Christine told us Larry threatened to kill you and the baby. You don't need to be afraid of Larry any more. I think he'll be going to jail for a long time."

Jody suddenly started to shake. "He'll get out and find me. Or he'll send someone to do it."

Mike went to her and took her hands in his. "Jody, I am a lawyer. I promise you that if you tell us the truth, and I mean everything whether you think it is important or not, I will do everything I can to help you. It is best that you not tell Christine, Ron or I any thing more about what has happened to you until you have told the police. But I will be with you all the time and if I think the police are doing anything that is not according to the law, I will stop all the questions. But if you lie to the police you will be in serious trouble."

Jody gave a loud cry and then began to weep silently. Mike just held her until she composed herself.

"I already lied to you."

Ron and Mike looked at each other.

"What lie did you tell, Jody?" Ron asked.

"When I said my dad made me get on the plane. He didn't say that. I thought I was going to become famous. Dad told me it wasn't too late to change my mind. But I thought it would be fun to be on TV."

Mike tried to suppress a slight smile. "Did you tell us any other lies?" he asked.

"No that's the only one. Will I have to go to jail now?"

"If you promise to tell no more lies I don't think you'll go to jail," he told her.

"I won't lie. I promise I won't. Can I take the baby and rock her now? I usually do this every morning."

"I think Bella would like that."

Christine was getting dressed when she heard the loud crying of Jody. But it stopped so suddenly she knew the men must have the situation under control. She quickly dried her hair and started to put on some lipstick when she heard the sound of a soft, sweet voice singing:

"O Danny Boy, the pipes, the pipes are calling,"…

Christine was stunned. The voice was very clear; every note was on pitch. *What a beautiful classical voice Jody has,* she thought.

"And I'll be here in sunshine or in shadow;
Oh Danny Boy, oh Danny Boy. I love you so!"

The melancholy sound of Jody's voice could soften the hardest of hearts Christine thought as she quickly made her way downstairs. She joined Ron and Mike who were staring in amazement at the young woman who now sat with her back to them rocking and singing to baby Bella.

"Jody," Christine said going to her. "I have never heard that song sung so well. It was truly, truly beautiful. You have a wonderful, wonderful voice."

Jody looked at Christine and said, "Thank you. It's a song I always sang to my little brother, Danny, when he'd miss our mother."

"Where was your mother?" Christine asked.

"She had a bout of cancer and I took care of the kids. But she's OK now."

"I bet she really misses you."

"I miss her. If the police say I can go home can I borrow enough money to take the bus home? I promise you my dad will send you the money back."

Christine knelt by her and wrapped her arms around Jody and Bella. "I'll make sure you get back home as soon as I can."

Jody laid the baby on a blanket on the floor and said she wanted to take a shower.

"Remember not to go into your old bedroom," Ron reminded her.

The ringing of the phone interrupted them. Christine answered it promptly.

"Hi, Christine. It's Elaine from across the street. Are you OK? We saw police cars at your place last night and they're back in the area today. There's a van from the television station parked down the street and a reporter from the newspaper out there. He's starting to knock on the neighbors' doors. Is there anything we can do to help you?"

"Elaine, I'm fine. I had some unexpected visitors staying with me and it seems one of them has gotten into trouble. I'm going to be okay. I'm so sorry the neighbors are being bothered."

"Well, the neighbors won't tell them anything because on our street we try to protect the privacy of people. But if you need any help or support please call us. Roy spent all night at the window with his cell phone in his hand. He said if he saw any car he didn't recognize in your driveway he would call the police. Please remember that we're here to help you if you need us."

"Thank you so much, Elaine. I will remember."

Christine flopped down into a chair with her arms hanging at her side. "There's a reporter going from house to house and a TV news van parked on the street."

"It's not a big deal, Christine," Mike told her. "They check the police blotter and are trying to get a story."

"You don't understand. My past will come back to haunt me. What if it becomes a big news story? This is something I have been afraid of for the last forty years."

"I don't understand, Christine," Ron told her. "A brief marriage to a jerk over forty years ago is not news."

"Not that marriage. My second husband was Leo Martinelli."

"You mean you were married to…" Mike started to ask.

Ron reached out and took her hand.

"George knew all about it before we were married. He always told me it was my story to tell or not tell. At first I didn't want to relive any old pain. Then, with the love of George and having him by my side, the subject didn't come up. I should have known it would follow me."

Mike spoke up. "As I remember that story on the news, you were a victim. The press reported that you were nearly dead for weeks. I never even suspected that person was you. As I remember it, the reporters hounded you relentlessly."

"For more than a year I was harassed by reporters and writers. After another couple of years I met George. After George and I got married, I had a new name and a new life. No one ever seemed to know or even suspect about my past. But maybe I fooled myself and now it will all come out in the papers."

"Christine, I'll try my legal best to keep the publicity down. If you like, I can act as your legal spokesperson. I may be able to control some of the coverage," Mike said. "A lot of time has passed. People may not even be interested."

"I'd like that, Mike. I don't think George ever imagined anything like all this happening when he asked your dad to look after me."

"Well, I know Ron will help me. Right, Ron?" he asked looking at him.

"You bet. But remember this, Christine: your friends and neighbors know the real you. For years and years you have been an important member of our community. I don't think our locals will let you down."

"Should Joe Sisi know? I don't want to make his job any harder."

"If you say it's okay, I'll give him some highlights so he won't get surprised by anything," Ron said. "I'm sure he'll be very discrete."

'I agree. He shouldn't get blindsided. Here they come to do a house search," Mike said as he looked out the window. "Why don't you bring Jody down here? I'll stay with her in case they try to question her. We'll let Joe ask the questions."

"Sounds like a good plan to me," Ron said as he went to answer the door.

Two officers came into the house. They presented the search warrants to Christine.

"Ron, please show us the room Mr. Parker occupied while he was here," one of the officers asked. "We'll start there."

"Where's Larry?" Jody asked the police officer as she came down stairs. "Will he be coming back here?"

"Jody, Larry has broken the law in many ways. I believe he will be in jail for a long time."

"Do you need me to go with you to the police station" Ron asked Christine as she prepared to drive Jody and Bella to the station. "Mike will be meeting you there."

"You've done so much already. I think I can manage this."

"Then I'll go home to change clothes and see you there. It may be difficult for Jody to give up the baby. She's been very protective of her."

"I guess I'll pretend I don't know anything about anything."

Chapter 18

When they got to the station a woman came into the room and took the baby. Joe came into the room with another man. He introduced Agent Mark Williams of the FBI. He asked Jody to sit across the table from them. Jody asked Christine to stay with her and Joe said she could because Jody was a minor. Mike came in to join them to represent Jody.

"I believe your name is Jody Stewart. Is that correct?" Joe started.

"No."

"What is your correct name?"

"Erin Parker."

Christine sat there dumbfounded but tried to remain quiet.

"How old are you?"

"Sixteen."

"The name of the man you were with is Donald Parker, not Larry Stewart. Is that correct?"

"Yes."

"Do you know the real name of the baby?"

"I guess it's Bella Parker since Donald is her dad."

"Is the baby your daughter?"

"No."

"Do you have any information about the baby? Where or when she was born?"

"No."

"Let's start at the beginning, Jody. Tell me about your first meeting with Donald Parker."

"His dad and my dad are some sort of cousins. Donald and his dad came to our home in Kentucky when I was about six or seven. I don't remember too much about the visit except they played their guitars and we all sat around and sang. We never saw them again but Donald's dad did start to phone us last summer, not very often though. Right after school was out for the summer this year, either Donald or his father called my dad and told him they were music and record producers and looking for a new young singer. They remembered me. At first my dad and mom said absolutely not but he kept calling. He said I could be a star with my first recording. He sent a plane ticket for me to come to Vegas. He said we'd make a recording and I'd be home in a few weeks; plenty of time before school starts in September."

Agent Williams interrupted to ask her for the day and month she flew to Vegas and the airline information.

"What happened when you got to Vegas?" Joe asked.

"Donald met me. He was carrying Bella. He said his wife had died when Bella was born and he took Bella everywhere. When we got to his car I saw it was filled with suitcases and boxes. He said we were on our way to a new recording studio in Seattle. When we stopped at night he slept in the bed and the baby and I slept on the floor. A day or so later he told me he needed more money. We'd stop at his aunt's house because she was very rich. He said she was an old, very sad woman. Her mom and dad had been killed in a car accident years ago and her little brother got in trouble and was in jail. But he said we must not tell her that. Instead he would tell her that his dad was her little brother. He told me from now on my name was Jody and he was Larry Stewart. When I told him I wanted to use my own name he slapped me and told me to shut up. I was so scared. Then he told me that if I didn't do everything he said to do, he would kill Bella and me. We were mostly driving in the country and I didn't know where I was. Aunt Tina, sorry, I mean Mrs. McCall, was very kind to us. I felt safer here. Donald was gone most of the day. At first I was afraid that Aunt Tina might hate me and the baby. But Aunt Tina was very good to me and tried to be nice. But I was afraid I might say something wrong so I tried to stay in my room."

"Do you know where he went during the day?"

"He said he was looking for day jobs to earn some money."

"I understand your plans to leave town came about very suddenly. Did he talk with you about it?"

"No."

"Did he always have the same car?"

"Yes."

"Do you remember it making any funny noises or seem to have any trouble."

"No."

"Did you think he was lying about the car breaking down?"

"I don't know much about cars so I didn't think about it. He kept telling me how much money he was going to have. One day I asked him why he needed his aunt's money if he was going to be making recordings. He reached over and slapped me again and told me to shut up."

"Did you meet up with his father or anyone else along the way?"

"I never saw him meet anyone."

"Let's talk about the baby. Did Donald ever tell you anything about Bella?"

"No. When I asked about what kind of baby food or formula she liked, he said any kind was okay. He told me to just buy anything. He didn't talk about Bella's mother."

"Erin, did Donald ever say he was Bella's father?"

She was quiet for a minute. "I'm not sure. I always thought her mother was dead but I don't know if he said those words. Maybe I just thought that. I didn't know what to do. I didn't know what to do," she repeated. She began to cry silently but quickly dried her tears and tried to appear brave.

"Erin, if you could, what do you want to do now? Stay in California? Return home?"

"I want to go home. Mrs. McCall said she'd help me with bus fare if you say it's okay."

"I'm not sure I can make that happen right now. But I can arrange for you to talk with your parents. Is that okay?"

"I'd really like to talk with them but I'm afraid they'll be mad at me."

"Maybe it would be best if I talk with them first. Then you can talk with them. After you do that, I want to talk with you again. Your cousin is in a lot of trouble. He has lied about many things. He has stolen things from Mrs. McCall and sold them. He has stolen license plates on his car to try to hide who he really is. You seem like a bright intelligent young woman. Even if it makes you sad, before you leave here I want you to know the whole truth. Why don't you write down your home phone number and I'll make the call." Joe gave her a pen and note pad and then left the room to make the call.

"Did I do okay?" Erin asked Christine and Mike. "How can I tell my folks what happened? They will probably hate me."

"I think they'll be glad to hear from you," Christine said.

"Why did the police take Bella? Do they think I hurt her?"

"It's probably a routine procedure," Mike told her.

After a brief period of time, Joe came back into the room. "We have confirmed what you told us about your flight to Vegas. You were very truthful. I've just talked to your dad. I told him about your ordeal. He is anxious to talk with you. He is very happy you are okay. He is going now to talk with your mother and they both will be on the line when you call them back. But before we do that, I need to tell you about Donald Parker. He is in a lot of serious trouble. He has told you and your family many lies. He is a very bad man. He is not in the music business.

He doesn't even have a job. He has a legal wife named Jane and two sons. He has no daughters. He does not see or support his family. He has been in trouble with the law, mostly minor things. But he does have a police record."

Joe took the papers he had with him and spread them on the table. Erin saw Donald's police mug shot and a sheet that listed his various crimes. She looked up at Christine in disbelief.

"I didn't know any of this," she told Joe. "I'm telling the truth. I didn't know any of this," she repeated. "I know my dad didn't know this."

"I believe you, Erin. But we haven't got to the bad part yet."

"Your father told me that Donald's father is Roger Parker. Roger and Christine went to school together. As soon as they graduated from high school they were married and left the home town because Roger was sure he could become a famous singer. He did many harmful and hurtful things to Christine. Christine left him and eventually divorced him. When Christine made a trip back home to West Virginia, she learned that her parents and little brother were killed in a car accident. No one knew for sure just where the accident occurred. After some years Christine met and married George McCall. They had a long and happy marriage before his death. George McCall was a very smart business man and left Christine enough money to take care of her for the rest of her life. It appears that Roger apparently learned about the money and shared Christine's story with his son, Donald. The FBI is questioning both men right now. It was Donald's or Roger's plan to pretend Donald was a long-lost member of Christine's family and then find a way to get her money. He used the story of making you a star to help convince Christine that he was a good family man."

"But I had no baby. Whose baby is little Bella?" Erin said as she shook her head back and forth in disbelief. "Or did he have a baby maybe with some other woman?"

"We have tested the DNA of both Donald and Bella. They are not relatives."

"But where did he get Bella?"

"We're almost sure Bella was kidnapped to be part of his plan."

Erin's face went pale. Her body went limp as she fell back into her chair.

"Kidnapped?"

"Yes," Joe answered quietly.

"Did he kill anyone?"

"Not that we know of at this time. Do you know if he carried a gun?"

"I know he had two. He hid one under the mattress of the bed at your house, Aunt Tina, and he always carried the other one with him. It was pretty small. I guess he carried it so he could kill me if I did something wrong."

"He did not have a gun when he was arrested." Joe told her.

"He put it in the glove compartment of Aunt Tina's car when he saw the police cars."

Christine felt herself start to shake. She held on to the edge of the table and hoped that no one would see her hands shaking.

"Is your car in the parking lot?" Joe asked Christine. When she indicated it was, he asked for her keys and immediately sent someone to retrieve the gun.

Erin seemed oblivious to everyone. She kept shaking her head.

"Bella…kidnapped? I don't understand," she said. "Don't people report kidnapping? Can't you find her parents? Bella needs her real dad and mom."

"We may be able to reunite the family very soon. Many children are reported missing. We have to be sure we find the real parents."

"Does it take a long time?"

"Sometimes it does. But we had a head start this time. Christine is a very smart woman. She could not quite believe that her little brother had survived the car crash all those years ago. She shared those concerns with Ron, who is an investigator. Ron took DNA samples from Donald and Bella. With that information on file we don't have to wait for test results when we find the parents. We believe it happened in the Vegas area since he had Bella with him when he met you at the airport. There was a report of a kidnapping in a nearby town the day before Donald met you. We are trying to determine if Bella is that baby. That baby was born in Arizona but the family moved to a suburb of the Las Vegas area shortly after her birth. In Arizona when a baby is born most hospitals make what is called an heirloom birth certificate. It is not a legal document but includes all the birth information along with a footprint of the baby. A copy of that form was faxed to us this morning. But the police in that town have already made an arrest in the case. The man arrested is a drifter in the area whose fingerprints were on the gate. So now every fact we have and every fact they have will have to be verified. While we have been talking, our lab did a footprint of Bella. It appears to be a match with the missing baby. But we don't have all the facts yet. Let me ask you another question. Did Donald give any indication of what day jobs he did to earn some money?"

"No," Erin said in a strong loud voice. "Is very much missing from your house?" she asked Christine.

Christine remained silent.

"We have located several items that were taken from her home and sold. We expect to find more." Joe looked at his watch. "It's time for you to talk to your parents. I have already told them what I just told you. They are anxious to know you are okay." He picked up the phone in the room and asked the agent to put the call through to Erin's parents. "You can talk as long as you like. Just knock on the glass when you're done." He motioned to Christine and they left the room together.

"Thank you for being so gentle with her," Christine told Joe. "Do you think her parents will welcome her home?"

"I think so. Her parents are in a state of shock right now but eager to talk with her. They are filled with guilt for letting her come west. When they didn't hear from Erin they contacted Roger who always told them Erin wasn't home to talk with them. They have been very worried about their daughter. They asked me how soon she can leave California. That will be up to the FBI and our legal department. She may have to give a deposition or maybe even need to testify in a trial. Her parents are now trying to arrange for one of them to come to be with her. I suggested they wait for a day or so. We will try to find her a place to stay while we sort things out."

Christine spoke up. "She can stay with me if you say it's okay. I hate the thought of her being alone. Can she go home with me now? She's been a victim too. But first, can you tell me the story about the baby?"

"In a little town about thirty miles from Vegas a mother and her three young children were playing in the fenced back yard of their home. Someone rang the doorbell. The mother went inside to answer it. It was a man trying to sell carpet cleaner. The mother quickly sent him on his way and returned to the back yard. Her baby was gone. The two-year old was playing. The oldest child who was four years old told the police that Santa Claus had taken the baby. There was a good set of fingerprints on the gate to the yard that matched those of a drifter in the neighborhood. The drifter admitted standing at the gate watching the children but denied taking the baby. He is still being held. The police had no other leads after a thorough investigation. We believe that Bella is that baby. Her footprint is a match with the one on the heirloom birth certificate. As we sit here now the FBI is on their way to her house with a picture of Donald Parker to see if the mother recognizes him as the salesman at her door. The parents had their DNA recorded at the time of the abduction. The FBI is comparing it now to the sample from the baby. We still can't explain for sure how the baby was stolen or the Santa Claus bit. I really believe we'll get the answers." Joe paused for a moment and seemed deep in thought. Then he turned to Christine and said, "If you hadn't shared your concerns with Ron and Mike about Donald being your nephew, I really believe things would have ended badly for you, for Erin, and for baby Bella."

Erin knocked on the glass window indicating she had finished her call and then came to join them.

"My mom and dad aren't mad at me. They want me to come home." she told them. "One of them is going to come to California to be with me."

"I'm glad you will have your family with you," Christine told Erin. She turned to Joe Sisi and FBI Agent Williams. "Could we leave now to get some lunch? It's been a hard morning for all of us."

"Can we take Bella with us?" asked Erin. "She must be so scared and hungry right now."

"You may leave but I'm afraid we must retain custody of the baby," she was told.

"But she needs someone to take care of her. She needs her lunch and it's almost time for her nap." Erin's face was full of concern.

"We have an experienced mom with her right now," Agent Williams told her. "Why don't you have lunch and then stop back here. Christine, while you're eating, update Erin about our search for Bella's parents. We may have located them already," he told Erin.

As they made their way to a coffee shop across the street from the police station Erin was very quiet. "How can they be sure they found Bella's real parents?" she asked Christine.

"They have many ways to verify who she is: DNA and footprints among others."

"I bet they'll hate me. I should have tried harder to make Donald tell the truth. I really was scared of him. How did Donald take her? Wasn't her mom taking care of her?"

Christine told her about the apparent abduction of the baby.

Erin was very quiet for a time. "I bet her mom and dad have been really worried. I know they really hate me for not asking Donald more questions. Do you think they will want me to go to jail?"

"Were you ever in trouble with the police back home?" Christine asked.

Aunt Tina, I mean Mrs. McCall, "Sheriff Wright knows me and he can tell you I have never been in trouble. He is the coach of our Cross Country Team. I was a runner." She paused and then said, "I guess I won't be able to go back to school now."

"Erin, why don't you call me Christine. I don't think you have done anything bad enough to be put in jail. I can honestly testify that you were very kind and loving to the baby."

"I'm going to miss her. I wish I could explain to her parents that I thought Bella was Donald's child. Do you think they'll let me explain anything to them?"

"I don't know, child. Let's eat lunch and then we'll check back with Joe and then head for home if we can."

"Can I stay with you until my dad or mom gets here?"

"Yes, of course. But I might make you sing for me," Christine said, trying to lighten the mood a little.

Joe, Ron, and Mike were waiting for them when they returned to the station. Joe spoke first.

"The FBI has confirmed that baby Bella is really Angela Jo Hopkins. They are notifying the parents right now. An FBI agent will be taking her home this afternoon. The baby's mother did confirm that Donald was the salesman who came to her door. We suspect Roger may have actually taken the baby but we have a few more items to confirm."

"Can I tell her goodbye?" Erin asked as the tears began to flow from her eyes.

"You can," Joe told her.

"Did Donald really take her just to try to fool Aunt...I mean Christine?"

"We believe so. We're still checking things."

"But Christine isn't some old woman who is going to die. How could Donald get her money?" She paused a minute, then with a look of awakening and astonishment said, "Oh, no, no, no. Do you think he planned to kill her? Oh, Aunt Tina," she began to cry hysterically.

Christine held her and let her cry.

After a couple of minutes, Erin began to calm down and then had another thought. "Maybe he planned to kill Bella and me too." She began to weep even harder.

Ron came to her, knelt down in front of her and took both of her hands in his. "Erin, none of us know or may ever know what Donald's plans might have been. But that is past now. You did the right thing when you told Christine about Donald's threats against you. I know it took a lot of courage for you to do that. You were very, very brave. You helped us with information that is going to make everyone safer. You took good care of Angela Jo and now she can grow up with her mother, father, brother and sister."

"The FBI expects to have a plane here within the hour to return the baby to her parents," Joe told her. "Would you like to go spend a little time with her until the plane gets here?"

"Oh, yes, yes. Can Aunt Tina come too so no one will think I'm going to hurt the baby?"

Joe looked at Christine who nodded her assent and then said, "Both of you come with me."

He led them to a small room at the end of a long hallway. There was a cot against the wall. A rocking chair was in the center of the room. The FBI agent who had taken the baby when they had arrived at the station was holding Angela Jo. She got up from the chair and placed the baby in Erin's arms.

"I'll give you a few minutes alone," she said. "I understand the plane is already on the ground."

"Are you going to be the one to take her back to her mom and dad?" Erin asked.

"Yes, I will have the pleasure of doing that." She left the room.

Erin took the baby in her arms and sat in the rocking chair. The baby woke up and reached her little hand up to touch Erin's face. Erin kissed the little hand and began to talk to her.

"Sorry I called you Bella. Your real name is Angela Jo. You are a little angel. You are such a good girl. Now you are going on a long airplane ride and when you get there you will see your real mother and father. You have a big sister and brother. They will be so happy to see you. You must be a very good little girl. When you see your real mama, I think you should say 'Mama' to her. She will take really good care of you."

Erin sat quietly rocking the baby and began to sing to her. Then she stopped singing and began to talk to her again.

"I really love you, little Angela. I might fight to keep you if I was older. But I'm not old enough to know what to do to make sure you're safe and happy. But someday I hope I'll have the chance to see you again. But maybe that's not best." She paused, looking at the baby with her fingers intertwined with the baby's little hand. "Yes, I know it's not best. I hope you are so young you will never have any memories of this time you have been away from your real mama."

Christine thought her heart would break as she remembered how good Erin had been to this baby who was a stranger to her.

The FBI agent came back into the room. "It's time for us to leave for the airport," she quietly told Erin.

Erin slowly stood and placed the baby in the arms of the agent. As they started to walk out the door Erin suddenly cried out, "Wait."

Erin reached inside her knit top and pulled out a gold cross on a chain from around her neck.

"I've never taken this cross off since my folks gave it to me when I was ten years old. Would you please give it to Angela's mother? Tell her I'm sorry I wasn't brave enough to tell someone about Donald. I really thought she was his daughter. I tried to keep her safe, clean, and healthy. Maybe her mother can give the cross to Angela some day when she's older so that Angela will always know someone loved her."

"I'll be sure to give her mother your message."

They left the room.

Christine took Erin in her arms and let her cry as if her heart was broken.

Chapter 19

Christine stood holding Erin close to her until Erin began to pull away. She looked at Christine and said, "I might have died if you hadn't believed me when I said Donald threatened me."

"You are a strong young woman. You would have managed somehow."

"I haven't been very good about going to church but I sure did pray a lot these last weeks. I was afraid that if I left without the baby Donald would kill her. She was so sweet and she smiled so often. Do you think she missed her mama?"

"I'm sure she did. We all get used to living a certain way. But just like you coped with a bad situation, she did too. It was good that you knew how to take care of her. Do you have sisters or brothers?"

"I have a brother named Bob who is fourteen, my sister Joan is eleven, and my little brother, Danny is six now. I wonder if they still look the same."

"Well, I hope you won't have to wait too long to find out," Christine told her.

They heard a knock followed by the door opening. Joe, Mike and Ron came into the room.

Joe spoke first. "Erin, you did a very good job of helping to bring about a happy ending. I'm sorry if we were a little rough with you about stealing the clothes. Our only thought at that time was to get you to a safe place away from Donald. Ron had already told us about Christine buying you the new outfit."

Mike then spoke. "Erin, I'm very proud of you. You spoke clearly and concisely and told the truth. I know you were good with the baby. I'll never forget hearing you sing to her."

Erin began to stand a little taller and even tried to smile a little.

"We do have a problem right now," Joe said, "but we may have a solution if you're interested."

"What's the problem and what's the solution?" Christine asked.

"The local press is demanding an interview," Joe began. "We want to spare you that ordeal today. Ron came up with a good idea." He turned to Ron and said, "It's your turn."

Ron began. "I've been made aware of a problem out at the VA Home that I must take care of today." He turned to Erin. "I wondered if you and Christine want to ride along with me. It will only take me a few minutes. I know Christine has some very special friends out there who have been very worried about not seeing her for the last couple of weeks. She usually goes to visit them once or twice a week. I know these men will enjoy seeing you,

Erin. Chuck has a bit of Irish blood in him. I know he would really enjoy hearing you sing, *Danny Boy.*"

"I do not want to meet with the press, especially today," Christine said. "Do you think it is necessary that I be there? The trip to see the guys sounds good to me. What do you think, Erin? Are you up for a little side trip before we go home?"

"Do they know about me? Will they hate me?" she asked.

"Christine brings smiles to these men when she visits. Any friend of Christine is a friend of theirs." Ron told her.

"Joe and I can handle the press today." Mike told them.

Erin said she would go.

Ron led them through a back corridor and into a garage where his car was parked. As they left the garage they could see a mob of people and cameras on the front steps of the police station. Joe and Mike were preparing to talk with the crowd.

In less than five minutes, Ron had them away from the station through a back street and on their way for the visit.

"I don't have any perfume on," Christine said.

"Is that important?" Ron asked.

"Those guys always try to guess what kind of perfume I have on. It's a game we play. But I didn't put any on today."

"You should have a perfume called *Escape* today," Erin told her with just a hint of a smile in her voice.

"That's a brilliant idea, Erin," Ron said. "Do they make one called *Escape?*"

"I don't think so but it sounds good to me." Erin paused and then asked, "Will I ever feel normal again? I feel so bad about not having little Bella, I mean Angela, with me. But a little bit of me feels better because I know someone else is taking care of her."

"You have been through a terrible ordeal," Christine said. "No sixteen-year-old girl should have to go through anything like you have just been through. But you did get through it. Each day will feel just a little bit easier. If you have a bad day, just accept it and realize tomorrow will be better."

When they arrived at the home, Ron left for his office and Christine and Erin made their way to find Mel, Chuck, Kenny and Bruce.

"Christine," the men called to her as she came in. "We thought you forgot us."

"That will never happen," she told them. "I've brought someone to meet you. Fellows, meet Erin. We've been having an adventure together. She's been visiting me from Kentucky but will be going home soon."

"There was a story about you in the paper today," Chuck told her. "Is it all true?"

"Oh probably not," Christine told them. "You know how the press likes to exaggerate. But tell me about what you've been up to."

"Well, we didn't go outside. We were stuck here," Bruce told her.

"How old are you?" Chuck asked Erin.

"I'm sixteen."

"I have a granddaughter who is sixteen. She plays the piano. Do you play the piano?"

"I had a few lessons but I don't play very well. I'd rather sing."

"Well, sing something for me."

"What kind of song would you like?"

"Something that I can understand the words. Some of these young singers today don't even know how to speak."

Erin looked at Christine.

"How about a good Irish song to make you cry?" Christine asked.

"That'll never happen," Chuck said.

Erin took the cue from Christine and began softly to sing her own sweet version of *Danny Boy*.

The four men sat there mesmerized as they listened to the haunting sounds of her clear, sweet voice. By the time she finished, some of the patients and guests at the home were standing in the doorway listening to her.

For once in his life Chuck did not retaliate with some sharp remark. He sat there quietly listening and then said simply, "Thank you. That was really beautiful."

Ron, who had stood there listening, came into the room and said it was time for them to leave.

"Will you come back, little lady?" Chuck asked Erin.

"Maybe, but I'll be going home soon," she answered.

Ron hurried them out of the building and into the car. "I thought we'd go to Eynon's Steak House. We can have a nice quiet dinner there away from the crowds."

"Why are you being so good to me?" Erin asked.

"Because you are a nice young woman. You have been through an ordeal. But you survived it and now you are a stronger person. The worst of it is now over. I expect Donald will be in prison for a long time. And probably so will his father. Donald now says the whole scam was thought up by his dad, but Roger is denying it. We'll have to let the courts decide."

"Will I have to go to court and testify against him," Erin asked Ron.

"It's too soon to think about that."

"Will I have to come back to California?"

"Perhaps, but no more talk about it until tomorrow. Let's go in and eat. I bet you are starved."

They had a quiet, elegant dinner.

"I've never eaten in such a nice restaurant," Erin told them. "That dessert was just wonderful. But I ate so much I'm feeling sleepy."

As the car approached Christine's house, they saw a crowd gathered in the street about four doors beyond Christine's.

"I wonder what's going on," Christine said.

"It's mostly TV and newspaper people looking for a story. The neighbors decided to treat them all to a picnic dinner in the street away from your house so you can get home quietly. You two get out of the car quickly and go in the house. If you pull down your window shades, the press might not even know you're home."

"Ron, did you plan this so we could rest up tonight?" Christine asked.

"Nope. It was your neighbor Elaine's idea. She called me and I agreed. The neighbors all said they'd be happy to help. We can pick up your car tomorrow. I'll call you later," Ron said as he sped away.

"I feel like I'm home," Erin said.

"I'm glad you feel that way. Would you like to watch some TV or play the piano?" Christine asked her.

"Would I be rude if I said I just want to go to bed?"

"Not at all. We both need to get some rest. It's nearly midnight in Kentucky but tomorrow morning you can call your folks and have a long talk with them."

"Could I really do that? I don't have any money for a call."

"My phone plan allows me to call anywhere for as long as I want so plan for a nice visit."

"Christine, you are really a very nice person," Erin said as she gave Christine a hug.

Christine made her way to her bedroom. *I think this day has been one of the longest days of my life. Oh, George,* she thought as she looked at his picture. *I have so much to tell you.* But she was asleep as soon as her head hit the pillow.

Chapter 20

When Christine woke early the next morning she saw the sun was already peeking around the window shades. She peered out the window and saw a TV van in front of her house. Elaine was already out serving coffee to the reporters. Christine waited until Elaine went inside and then phoned her.

"What a wonderful surprise you gave me. Thank you so much. I don't think I could have talked with anyone last night."

"Christine, you have been so good to all your neighbors. Any time we get a sneeze or a sniffle you are right there to help us. You never let it show but you must have been under a terrible strain the last few weeks. We decided to be nice to the press and not kick them out so that maybe you could have a few minutes to recoup. Ron called to tell me the plan worked well."

"It certainly did. I'm dreading it but I may need to meet with the press very soon. I haven't read any papers lately but I imagine that the whole story is there. A young man with a connection to my first husband came here pretending to be the son of my dead brother. Along the way he coerced a young distant cousin with a scam to become famous and he kidnapped a baby. But the baby has been taken back to her parents."

"I can't believe all that happened on our street without any of us knowing about it."

"If I had known the truth, I probably would have been crying on your doorstep," Christine told Elaine. "I do want you to know how much I appreciate all that you are doing for me. I'll owe the whole block a party."

Christine peeked in on Erin who was still sound asleep and made her way to the kitchen. She heard a knock on the kitchen door. It was Mike.

"I brought you the keys to your car. The police brought it home last night. I thought I'd update you on what happened after you left the station. The press wanted to talk with you but Joe told them I was representing you. I told them you had been married at age seventeen and divorced the next year. You heard about the death of your parents and brother but you had been unable to confirm it. I told them how Donald, using the name of your dead brother, arrived in town claiming to be the son of that brother. In spite of your wanting to believe him; you had lingering doubts which you shared with Ron and me. From little bits of information you were able to obtain we contacted Joe Sisi of the Crofton PD. We were able to identify Donald as the son of your ex-husband. Then Joe took over the briefing and told them about Erin and the baby, and that Baby Bella, as we knew her, is now reunited with her real parents. The rest of the interview was not about you, but about the kidnapping which Joe talked about."

"Do you have any more information about the kidnapping?" she asked.

"Let me show you a picture of the man we're almost certain took the baby." He laid a police mug shot of a man who looked very, very old or someone who had been very, very sick. The man's face was thin and gaunt. He had long stringy yellow-white hair that fell far below his shoulders. He had a white scrawny beard and yellowed teeth. Another full length picture of the man showed the hair and the beard extended well below his waist.

"Is this the man that took the baby?" Christine asked, "The man the older child said was Santa Claus? I can see why a child might say that."

"This is the man," Mike said. "Do you recognize him?"

"I've never seen this man before in my life."

"Are you sure?"

Christine stared at the picture. She quietly looked up at Mike and asked, "Is this a picture of Roger Parker?"

"Yes."

"But he looks so terribly old."

"He is sixty years old."

"Has he admitted to taking Angela?"

"He claims to know nothing about the kidnapping or his son's visit to see you. He calmly asked how you were, where you live, and so on. He said he and Donald do not stay in touch. He says he is innocent of any part in the scheme. However, Erin's father has already told the police about Roger calling him to try to get Erin to go to Vegas.

Roger is denying that he made any phone calls. The FBI is holding him now."

"This makes me so very, very sad. He was a lazy jerk looking for someone to take care of him, but I can't believe he'd stoop this low." Christine sat quietly for a couple of minutes then asked Mike, "Do you think he really meant to kill me?"

"We may never know for sure. I'm hopeful there are enough charges to keep him in jail for a long, long time."

Christine and Mike sat quietly for a few minutes. Then she asked, "Do you know what is going to happen to Erin? Will she face any charges?"

"Probably not but it may depend on what story Roger comes up with. He may try to say her dad called him for help to make her a singing star. Things are still a bit unsettled. Right now, Roger will say nothing to even help his son so who knows?"

"Will Erin be allowed to go home?"

"I'm almost positive she will. That's another thing we need to talk about." Mike looked at his watch. "Her parents should be arriving in California about now. They are really angry with themselves for letting Erin leave home. I arranged for my firm's plane to meet the plane from Kentucky at the San Francisco airport and fly them here to Crofton. Ron plans to meet the plane here and bring them to the police station. Joe wants to meet with them before they see Erin. He would like you to bring Erin there around 10:30. Will this be a problem for you?"

"Of course not, but I'd better get some groceries in the house and tidy up a bit. Erin is going to be so happy."

"Don't worry about your house. Joe had told them not to come for a couple of days because he planned to check a few more facts and then put her on a plane for home. But they couldn't wait. They want to see their daughter."

"I guess it's not easy to be a parent," Christine said.

"Most parents just try to do the best they can," Mike answered.

Chapter 21

Christine decided she'd let Erin sleep until around nine. She checked her food supply and found she had plenty of food on hand. She went upstairs and made up the bed in the third bedroom with fresh bedding. She wanted to have a place where Erin's parents could rest. She finished up and since it was only 8:30, she decided to call Betty. After all, she now had no relics to take for the Civil War Dinner.

"Christine, I'm so glad you called," Betty told her. "We have been so worried about you. Are you OK now? Can we do anything to help? Ray has been so worried that my call to you the other morning might have put you under a lot of additional pressure that you didn't need."

"Actually, Betty, I think your call helped us to bring an earlier end to the ordeal. I asked Larry, as we called him then, if he'd help bring those Civil War relics down from the attic. He suddenly decided they needed to leave. I knew I needed to keep him in town because Ron and Mike were working on information constantly. As much as I wanted him out of the house instantly, I also wanted to know who he was. I guess there was still a tiny bit of hope in my heart that he was a true relative. I urged him to stay for a few more days by telling him I wanted to give him some money to make his move to Seattle go smoothly. All the pieces started to fall into place when Ron and Mike found he had been spooked by my asking him to go to the attic. Actually, that's why I'm calling you now. I'm afraid that he has taken everything of value from the attic and sold it. I will have nothing to use at the dinner. I'm so sorry."

"Well, I'm sorry you had to go through such an ordeal. Old relics matter so little after what you've been through. What is most important is that you are safe now. We will come up with an alternative plan."

They chatted a few more minutes and then Christine went to awaken Erin. She decided to let her be surprised when she saw her parents. *They must be very worried about their daughter. They didn't waste any time in getting here,* she thought.

She knocked gently on Erin's door. "Time to wake up sleepyhead," she called into the room. "Come on downstairs and have some coffee or hot chocolate."

"That's the best sleep I've had since I left home," she said sleepily.

"We're going to have a busy day so we don't have a lot of time this morning."

"Is it okay if I call my folks?"

"Why don't you wait? Joe wants to see you at 10:30 this morning to tie up a few loose ends."

"Can I turn on the radio in the bedroom or will it bother you?"

"Of course you can turn it on. Turn it up full blast if you want," Christine told her. Christine just stood and thought for a minute of how intimidated this young girl had been when she arrived. *I hope she can recover quickly.*

A few minutes later they were on their way to the station.

"I wonder what questions Joe will have for me today," she said. "I wonder how long I'll have to wait before I can go home. You've been so good to me but I really miss my family. I bet the kids have grown a lot. Danny was learning his ABC's and my brother Bob was practicing to try out for the football team."

"We'll know very soon," Christine told her. "There's Joe waiting for you at the end of the hallway."

"Can you stay with me?" Erin asked Christine.

Joe smiled at Christine and then said, "Erin, there's a surprise for you in the room." He opened the door for her and then closed the door and walked to Christine. "I think we have a very happy reunion taking place in there right now. I'm going to release her as soon as the reunion is over and they'll be free to return to Kentucky. The parents told me the same story Erin told me. We may need more information from her in the future but we have no need to detain her."

"I know she wants to go home. She's been through a lot." Christine paused and then said, "Joe, how can I ever thank you for saving my life. This whole episode is beginning to settle in on me now."

""It's another day at the office for me," Joe said. "It's really Ron and Mike who did all the leg work. It's nice to see a good end to a case."

"Is Roger admitting to his part in this scheme?"

"He's still denying everything but our evidence is strong."

"Do you think I'll have to testify?"

"You might have to but most likely all legal proceedings will be in Nevada. It's too soon to know yet."

Ron and Mike came to join them as they sat on a bench outside the room where Erin and her family were talking.

"Are things getting quieter now?" Ron asked.

"Yes. As soon as they have a couple of more minutes, I'm going to go in and tell them they can all leave," Joe told them.

"Then I'll take them all home until they get ready to return to Kentucky," Christine told the men.

Joe spoke up. "The first time I talked with them on the phone, I suggested they give me a couple of days before coming to California. I was pretty certain that we'd be releasing Erin quickly, but they were very worried. They got the first plane they could to be with her. They're very embarrassed about letting her come west alone. They thought it was only for a month or so. When they didn't hear from her they were very worried and contacted Roger who told them she was just very busy. He said he'd tell her to call them. At the end he stopped returning their calls. In spite of this, Roger is still denying that he knew anything about the whole affair."

"What will happen to Roger and Donald?" Christine asked.

"They both are looking at some hard time," Joe told her.

Erin opened the door and motioned for them all to come into the room to meet her parents. Their eyes were red and their cheeks were stained with tears yet there was calmness and a look of joy on their faces as they looked at their daughter. *I'm glad Erin has family to care for her,* Christine thought.

"I'm Christine and I'm very happy to meet you," she said as she reached out to shake hands with Erin's parents, but the parents reached out to embrace and thank her for helping to keep Erin safe. Mike and Ron were introduced. Joe then spoke up.

"Erin, I have some good news for you. You are free to go back home to Kentucky. I told your folks that I doubt we will need to have you come back. You have been through a very, very bad experience but you proved yourself to be a strong young woman and wise beyond your years. You saved the baby's life by taking such good care of her and you saved the lives of Christine and yourself by being brave enough to tell Christine about Donald. I know you will probably never forget this experience but I hope you try to let it go in your mind and think about all the good things in life that are waiting for you. If you ever have questions that you think about, feel free to call me at any time. You are young and strong and beautiful. You have parents who love you. And you have friends in California who will never forget you. I know you can have a wonderful life."

Erin went to him and gave him a hug. "I'll never forget you."

Christine then invited them all to her home. "I fixed up the guest bedroom so you can rest a while. You must be exhausted."

"We can't trouble you," Erin's mom said. "We'll go to a motel."

"Actually, going to Christine's house is probably a better idea. The motels and hotel have many reporters waiting to question anyone new in town. Christine has an army of neighbors protecting the house," Ron told them.

Erin's dad then spoke up. "I'm going to try to get us booked on a plane to go home as quickly as possible. Your offer is very gracious. Thank you."

"I don't want to cut your visit to California short," Mike began, "but I have an offer for you to consider. The plane that brought you from San Francisco to Crofton belongs to my firm. I arranged to have it waiting for you. I just learned that early tomorrow morning the plane is scheduled to fly to Washington D.C. If you're ready to leave that quickly there is room for you. The pilot could take you to Lexington or Louisville if you're interested."

"That's like an answer to a prayer," Erin's mom said. "We had to leave the other kids with neighbors. They are so lonesome to see Erin. Getting home so quickly would be wonderful."

Mike said he wanted to take everyone for lunch. As they were leaving the police station the young woman from the FBI who had taken baby Angela Jo to her parents came rushing into the room. "One of the guys at the desk told me you were still here."

Erin introduced her parents to the agent.

"I have a message for you from Angela Jo's mom and dad. We don't give out anyone's address without permission from that person, so they gave me their address and asked me to give it to you. They hope you will contact them so they can express their thanks and gratitude to you for caring for the baby." She reached out her hand. "They wanted me to give this to you."

She handed Erin a gold cross on a chain. "When I gave them your cross for Angela Jo, her mother told me she will keep it until Angela Jo is ten years old and then give it to her. She was really touched by your thoughtfulness. From her own neck she removed this cross which was given to her when she was ten. She never took it off before, but she wants you to have it to remember Angela Jo."

Erin stood staring at the cross she held in her hands. "Mom…Dad…"

Her mother reached out and took the cross and placed it around Erin's neck. "Now you will always have a bit of Angela Jo with you."

Chapter 22

The house seemed so terribly quiet when Christine woke up. There were no sweet baby sounds coming from the other bedroom. Christine could hardly believe that the previous weeks had passed so quickly. At the time, some of the days had seemed very long. But now, Erin and her parents were back in Kentucky, Angela Jo was with her parents in Nevada, Donald was going back to Las Vegas to stand trial, and Roger…well, he was in jail also. She had very little time to spend with Erin's parents but perhaps that was just as well. It was not a good idea to prolong the visit. Everyone needs to get back to normal as quickly as possible. Christine then began to think about herself. Her mornings of exercising and planning seemed to be a thing of the past. She thought about all the things she needed to do. The whole house needed a good cleaning, there was a stack of laundry to be done, and the refrigerator was empty. But it felt good just to lie and rest a while.

She had been so busy trying to find out if Larry/ Donald really was her relative that she had not given any thought to the fact that she might be in danger. And especially in the kind of danger that led to death. She'd had no time to think about it while it was happening, but now as she did think about it she began to shake and then to cry. But after about five minutes of agony she began to realize how many good people were in her life. Ron and Mike were by her side from the first mention of the visit of her so-called nephew. The people from her church sent notes and treats. Her neighbors were wonderful as they watched out for her and kept the press away. *I refuse to lay here and feel sorry for myself. I have work to do.* She got out of bed, put on her jeans and decided to give the house a good cleaning and then make a list of the many people she wanted to thank for their support. She must find a way to thank some of them individually.

She was busy at work when the doorbell rang. She opened the door to find Joe Sisi and one of his staff. They had with them many of the items that had been stolen from her attic.

"We made a raid of all the second-hand and antique stores in town. Using the list you gave us we have been able to locate and return some of the items. We'll keep looking for the rest. Some had been sold so we have to locate the buyer," Joe told her.

"Thank you so very much. I probably will never know how you managed to do so much so quickly but I know I owe my life to you," Christine told him.

"It was amazing how calm and cool you stayed through the whole thing," he told her. "We kept our priorities straight. Most important was your safety, then the lives of the baby and Erin. If you had not stayed calm, who knows what Larry/Donald would have done?"

"I will be forever in your debt. You are a good man, Joe Sisi."

After he left Christine began to shake and cry again as she thought of the danger she had been in. But after a few minutes, she dried her tears and began to look at the items Joe had returned.

I never expected to see any of these things again, and yet here they are. I'd better let Betty and Ray know. She hurried to the phone to give them the good news.

"I know I've been absent from your meetings, but you must let me know how I can help with the dinner. It will be good for me to get back to the routine of my old life," she told Betty.

"Actually," Betty told her, "I'm so glad you called. I didn't want to bother you with a call. You have been through so much. But our committee met and decided since we might not have your special items, we should change our plans. We decided to postpone the Civil War dinner until spring. We are going to have our Round-the-World dinner this fall. I was surprised to learn many people in town have come from other countries. We are finding a lot of interest and support. I hope you're not disappointed."

"Of course not," Christine said. "Tell me about the new plans."

"We're planning the dinner for the middle of September. We hadn't realized until we got started how many different nationalities we have living in town.

Everyone wants to help and be a part of it. We're going to set up each of the five continents in a separate area with food, relics, history and maps and books about the area. Some people asked if they could attend wearing their native garb. We are encouraging them to do so. Oh, yes, there's something else I must tell you. We were asked if someone could wear an outfit from an earlier period of history. To be specific, there is a move on to get Joe Sisi to come dressed in a short tunic, sandals, and a gold wreath on his head like an early Roman warrior. Joe was asked about it and said 'Absolutely not,' but a money offer was made to him for the center he's trying to open. Other people pledged money to help him if he'll wear that outfit. Since we're only asking a fee for the gala of enough money to cover the supplies and space, this is a chance to help him out so we said yes. I hope you don't mind."

"I think it's a great idea. I didn't know Joe until this last ordeal I went through. He certainly would look the part. He's a big man with a lot of muscles. What sort of center is he trying to open?"

"I believe it's to be a youth center with spaces for sports and games and a section set aside for the kids to do homework and receive some tutoring."

"I think everything sounds just great. What can I do to help?"

"If you're up to it so soon, will you help to oversee the various menus for the food we'll serve? Are we pushing you too soon? One reason we postponed the Civil War dinner, which we plan to have in the spring, is because we definitely need you to oversee the food."

"Don't worry about me. I'll be fine. Getting busy again is going to be the best therapy for me."

As she hung up from that phone call, she received a call from Elaine across the street to make sure she was okay. That was followed by a call from Mike who wanted to be sure she was doing well and said his wife was insisting that she come for dinner that night. Then she had a call from Erin's mother thanking her once more for her hospitality and taking care of Erin. That call was followed by a call from Ruth King at the VA saying she was calling to check on Christine for their special friends. They urged her to come back as soon as possible. By now it was nearly lunch time and she had not finished her cleaning. *I'll have to get busy after lunch,* she thought.

The doorbell rang. It was Ron carrying a bag of food from McDonalds. "I didn't know what you like so I brought some of everything," he told her.

"I have been surrounded by so much love that I'm not sure I'll ever be able to repay everyone," she told him.

"Oh, we'll get even," he said with a laugh. "You might even have to start cooking again. Henry and Ed said they feel like they've been on a diet without your food."

As they sat in her kitchen eating their burgers and fries, Christine spoke. "I had a pity party for myself today," she told him. "For some reason for a while every few minutes I seemed to have a breakdown of sorts about what might have happened to me. I never thought I'd be afraid to face death, but somehow every time I thought of what might have happened I start to cry."

"That's not a pity party. You had no time to think before but now the pressure of everything is setting in. Just cry when you feel like it. These feelings will pass. If they don't there are a lot of people who will help you."

"How did you get so wise, Ron? I know so little about you. How did you get into the investigation business?"

Glad for a chance to change the subject, Ron began. "When I was in college, computers came on the scene. I was fascinated and loved them. I had a job with the security area of a big department store. I followed shoplifters around and learned how they work before I pulled them in for arrest. With the money I earned I bought my first computer. I soon learned the sneaky ways computers can be used for theft purposes. I got a summer job with a computer firm but realized my real interest was in using the computer to trace crooks. After I graduated I got a job doing just that. Soon my company loaned me out to other firms. I decided to quit my job and create my own company. When my wife wanted to come back to Crofton to be near her parents, I gladly made the move. Most of my work could be done from any base. We had a good life. I loved my work and made many friends all over the country. After my wife died, I was very lonely. I felt very old. I sold the house, moved to the retirement community, and then sold my company. I started to settle in on *old age*. Being a part of this investigation for you has led me to think I retired much too soon. It was good to stimulate my brain again."

"I don't know how I can ever repay you for keeping me sane through a very difficult time. I hope you'll send me a bill," Christine told him.

"I should send you a payment for helping me come alive again. I really had lost interest in everything. My daughter urged me and then pushed me to volunteer at the VA center. It helped me feel better. I really do feel younger these days. Now I've been asked to help on another case for a firm I used to do business with."

They sat quietly for a few minutes and then Ron said he had to leave. "Lunch has been fun but I really did come on a mission today. Remember when we located the burial place of your parents, I told you about the lady who had saved official records and items she retrieved from the accident. She saved them in a box."

"I remember you telling me that she thought I would come looking for information," Christine added.

"Yes, that's the woman. Well, I have the box with me in the car. I'll go get it." He went to his car and returned quickly with a medium size box, carefully sealed to keep out the dust. "Mike and I thought we might need to open it to help figure out what Donald was up to, but things moved so quickly it was not necessary. When you're ready, take your time to go through it. It may help give you some closure." He told her goodbye and went on his way.

Christine carefully opened the box. It seemed to be filled with bags. The woman had carefully sorted out items and saved them. One bag had what appeared to be copies of the official accident report. Another had newspaper articles about it. The official copies of the family birth and marriage certificates had been found in the car and were in another bag. In a small box Christine found her parents wedding rings. She found pictures and other treasures that her folks had been taking with them as they made their move from West Virginia to Nashville. She began to lay out the items on her kitchen table. She wanted to go through each one carefully. She found little remembrances from the funeral services. She carefully looked at them. She saw the name of the funeral home and the name of the cemetery where her family was buried: The Spring Garden Cemetery. That name rang a bell in her mind. But why? She laid it aside and returned to the box. Included was a child's book, *The Little Engine That Could*. The one she had given her little brother. The one she had read to him so many times. The same story that Donald used to try to convince her she was his aunt. She shook her head and placed the book on the table. After she sorted through the things she began to look carefully at each item. Then she remembered she was supposed to have dinner with Mike and his family. She made rows of everything on the table. *Tomorrow,* she thought. *I'll read each item tomorrow.*

Chapter 23

The next week she put her house back in order, worked on menus, visited her VA friends, cooked and took food to Ed and Henry. Each day she took time to carefully look at one envelope from the box of items from the accident. She read the newspaper reports about it. A large semi-truck had apparently lost its brakes and run her parent's car off the road and continued on down the mountain where it hit another car. Both drivers were killed. It wasn't until the next day when the police returned to take measurements and complete their investigation, that they followed the tracks from the truck back up the hill and then saw her family's car in a ravine. She came across the name of the cemetery again. Then she had an idea. She called Ron. "Are you too busy to take on a job for me?" she asked him.

"Might cost you a piece of pie," he told her. "What's going on?"

"When I went through *the box* the name of the cemetery stayed with me. Is it possible to find out on the computer if it's the same place my grandparents are buried?"

"A lot of cemeteries have that information on line. Give me the name of the cemetery and your grandparents' names and I'll check it out."

About ten minutes later, Christine's phone rang. Ron gave her the names and dates of her various relatives who were buried there.

"I can't believe that my family is buried with my mother's family. It makes me feel so good to know that they are buried together. Thank you, Ron, for helping me to have closure for something I worried about for more than forty years. Some day I'm going to go back and visit the area. One more thing, Ron. Will you ask your friend Deke if he noticed anything the town particularly needs? I want to do something to say thank you to the town."

"As a matter of fact I asked Deke that already. He said there is a fund raiser going on to restore the town hall. He also said he saw shingles on the ground from the roof of a nearby church. Do you want me to get more information?"

"I'd appreciate that. I must try to find some way to repay the town for the kind way they took care of my family. See if Deke has any suggestions."

Christine tried to think of how she could say thank you to the many, many people who, without her even knowing about it, stepped up to help her. She thought about her neighbors who were so protective of her. She went to her phone and called Betty asking her to set aside fifty tickets for the Round-the-World soiree. She would give a set to each of the neighbors on her block along with a thank you note.

She thought about Ron, Mike and Joe, without whom she might not have survived. When she told Mike to bill her for the hours he spent, he had a fit, saying she was his friend. But she had to do something. Ron kept insisting he'd settle for a piece of pie and Joe reminded her that he was only doing his job and he was not allowed to accept any gifts. But she had to do something. Didn't she hear that Joe is trying to get a youth center started? Maybe that's an opportunity for her to help. Once her mind got started along the giving line, it became easier. After all, Mike had told her she needed to start giving some money away. She had more to spend that she ever thought she'd see in her lifetime. She got another idea. She went to the phone, called Eynon's Steak House and made reservations for six for that weekend. She phoned Joe and Mike and invited each of them, and their wives, to join her for dinner. Then she called Ron.

"Ron, do you have a special lady in your life?" she asked him.

"Just you. Why do you ask?"

"Well, then you can settle on me for a date. I want you to join Mike and Joe and their wives and me for dinner at Eynon's this weekend. Are you free to go?"

"You bet," he told her.

Christine breezed through her work the next few days with a smile on her face and in her heart. She hoped she'd be able to pull everything off to her satisfaction. She called Eynon's to make reservations. She asked for the manger and requested a table for six in a secluded corner so they had some privacy. She wanted an assortment of appetizers and wine brought to the table as soon as the guests arrived. She wanted each person to order his or her own entrée and she wanted a light beautiful desert brought at the end of the meal without being ordered. She wanted no mention made of who was paying for the dinners; the manager should charge her account. She wanted a quiet, peaceful time. They had all been through a lot.

Christine had fun getting ready to go out. She put on a black sheath dress, added a gold chain with a diamond around her neck and, of course, her extremely high-heeled shoes. She carefully applied her makeup, gave her bright red hair a toss and took another look in the mirror. "Do I look okay, George?" she asked him. Satisfied with her appearance she got downstairs just as Ron arrived at the door to drive her to the restaurant.

"Wow," he said as he saw her. "You look absolutely fabulous."

"I know," she said with a haughty wave of her hand. "It's just a few old rags I put together at the last minute."

They both began to laugh and made their way to the door.

Joe and his wife, Gina, and Mike and his wife, Pat, were waiting for them. A beautiful selection of appetizers was on the table and the maitre'd was pouring each of them a glass of wine.

"A toast to a courageous, beautiful lady," Joe proposed.

The dinner was delicious and everything went well. As they were having desert and coffee Christine began to speak.

"I want to make a speech," Christine said. "I am here tonight because the three men here took my concerns seriously and helped me through a very bad time. I have tried to think of how I could let you know how much I appreciate what each of you did to keep me safe. As you know I'm helping on the Around-the-World dinner. I heard something interesting about you, Joe. I heard there is a movement to get you to come wearing, well, wearing almost nothing."

"Oh, Christine, don't embarrass me. I'm not going to appear in public wearing a Greek tunic with a wreath around my head," Joe said with a laugh.

"If I donated $25 to your Youth Center Fund would you do it?"

"Nope."

"How about if I give you $50?"

"Nope."

"How about $100?" Christine looked at Mike and asked, "I can afford $100 can't I?"

"Yes, you can afford $100," Mike told her.

"Great. Then it's settled." She reached into her purse and pulled out a check and handed it to Joe. Joe took the check, looked at it and then showed it to his wife.

"I-I-I can't believe this," he told the others in a stuttering voice "It's a check for $25,000. I don't know what to say. I'm stunned."

"Joe, I know you cannot accept payment for what you did for me. So I'm happy to help support your new center. You will be helping many children. What better way is there for me to use the money George left me? Mike and I talked it over and decided you needed at least that amount to get started. When you find out what special needs you have, I will be happy to fund those for you."

Joe and Gina both got up from the table and came to give Christine a hug. The tears were flowing from Gina's eyes. "He has wanted to open a center ever since he joined the police department. You are making his dream come true," Gina said.

"I think he will be making the dreams come true for a lot of old women like me who think it will be fun to see him dressed in his short skirt at the dinner," Christine said with a smile.

Then she turned to Mike. "You told me you would not bill me for the hours you spent keeping me safe and listening to me cry. Ever since George died you have been there for me, keeping me safe and sane, and also keeping me in money. What can I do for a man like that? Together with your friend and law partner, Pete, we came up with a little something for you." She handed him an envelope.

"Christine," he said rather shyly. "You don't have to do anything. You and George were so much a part of my parent's lives that you are family to me." He opened the envelope. "Christine, Christine, what an honor you have given me," he said. Turning to the others he said, "She has given me an endowment at the university."

"When Pete and I began to talk, we thought about endowing a chair there, but as we talked on we thought about the research center they are trying to develop, also the full scholarships they need, and many other uses for the money. Pete and I thought the choice should be yours to make. After all, your name will be on it for at least a few years. You can work with Pete on the distribution."

"Christine, I think you might have finally brought me to tears," Mike said. "You are truly a great lady."

"Is it time for my slice of pie now?" Ron asked. "That's what I told you that you owed me."

"I didn't know what kind of pie to make so you have to settle for this tonight." Christine handed him a small package and an envelope. Ron laid the envelope aside and opened the package. He began to laugh with real delight. "Hey, this is exactly what I need," he said as he looked at his new iPad. "Now I can be professionally organized. This is the latest model. What a thoughtful gift. It will help me stay up to date on the new electronic tools of the trade." He turned to the others and said, "Helping Christine makes me think I retired too early. I won't go back to full time work but this tool will help me so much on the occasional jobs I might take." He laid it aside and reached for the envelope.

Christine spoke to the others. "Ron and I only became friends recently when he asked me about visiting his special friends at the VA Center. I had such a good time that it began to open up my life. I didn't realize until recently how I had shut myself behind closed doors after George died. I went through all the motions without ever realizing what I was doing. The biggest pleasure I got out of life was to go to the ocean, sit on a rock and talk to George. If you were to have asked me how I actually spent my time I couldn't have told you. My life was like my house. I swept and dusted but kept the curtains closed. I was shocked when I had such an outpouring of support from my neighbors and friends at church. They told me how much I had helped them in the past. But, truthfully, I don't remember any of it. After Ron introduced me to his special friends at the VA center, I discovered that I needed them as much as they needed me. We made a difference in each other's lives. What can I give to the man who brought me back to the living and in the process saved my life?"

Christine's guests sat quietly at the table listening to her speak. Ron had held the envelope in his hand, and finally said, "Well, I guess I'd better open this."

He opened the envelope. Inside were sketches of a wooded garden area with a tall fence around it. He looked at Christine with a question in his eyes.

She spoke. "Ron, those are preliminary plans for the 'Ron Davis Garden' at the VA Center. You know how much the patients like to go outside. But there is not enough help there to take the patients for regular outings. If they just open the doors some of the patients might wonder away from the area. I found out the grounds include almost another acre that is mostly a wooded area. I am funding a project to develop the land, leaving most of it with trees, but with cement paths for wheel chairs and benches for someone to rest along the path. The plans call for a ten foot high chain link fence around the perimeter to keep everyone safe. It is to be called the Ron Davis Garden. I hope you won't mind the extra work to help plan it for I want you to make the final decisions."

Ron sat there totally in a state of shock. "I don't know what to say," he finally uttered. "Christine brought those men back to life. She is a stranger to no one. The men all love her and agonized for her during her last ordeal. These men gave up a normal life while serving the country. They ask for so very little. It will be an extreme honor for me to be a part of something as grand as this. Thank you, Christine."

Everyone was quiet for a few minutes.

The maitre'd sent coffee to the table and then came to see what else they might need or want.

Joe spoke up and said, "This has been a magical dinner. I don't think there is anything else any of us need tonight."

Chapter 24

Christine sat at the table with a cup of coffee looking at her to-do list. She had to make a decision soon about whether or not to go to France for the winter. Mimi and Bob Simpson had called her when they heard the news about her past life coming to haunt her. This couple who had introduced Christine to George owned a house in the south of France where she and George spent their honeymoon. Bob was one of George's best buddies. Now Bob and Mimi thought she should get away and come to spend the winter with them. Christine knew it was very beautiful at the old farm house. If she walked for a mile she'd be able sit on a cliff that overlooked the blue Mediterranean. She and George loved it there. These dear friends were both in their eighties now and didn't like to travel very far from home. They said their daughter, Jeannine, who was Christine's age, would meet her in Paris; rest for a day or so, and then drive them south. A few months ago Christine might have made immediate plans to go. But now she didn't know if she really wanted to go. The way her friends had rallied around her during her ordeal made her feel like she had a real family now. Neighbors stopped in for coffee. She felt welcome to stop in their homes at any time. The neighbor kids all called out to her when she saw them in the grocery store or on the street. Word had gotten out about her support for Joe's youth center and many other people also made donations to help. The Round-the-World dinner was less then two weeks away. So many tickets had been sold that they had to move it to the Conference Center at the nearby community college. Christine felt good about her life. *For so many years I worried that the story of my life with Leo would come back to haunt me. Yet, it turned out to be my life with Roger that made public all my secrets.* The whole thing seemed really bizarre to her.

She wondered if Roger had ever admitted his part in the scheme to scam her. The last she heard he was still denying that he knew anything about it. She wasn't sure if she even wanted to know. *Yes, I do,* she thought. *I know he was involved. He must not, he must not, he must not get away with it.* She decided to call Joe Sisi to ask him if he had any updated information.

"Christine, it's nice to hear from you. I was about to call you. It seems Roger is still denying any involvement in the scheme. He refuses to talk with his son, Donald. Donald still says his dad did the actual kidnapping of Angela Jo. Roger says he wants to talk with you but we're not going to give him that luxury. A preliminary hearing is scheduled for next week. The DA there wants you, Ron, Mike and me to be there to be deposed for the trial. It is their hope that they will not have to make Erin or

Angela Jo's parents come to testify but it may be necessary. I talked with Mike this morning. He'll be calling you."

Christine ended the call full of rage and fury. "Roger, you snake," she said very loudly. You can't scam me any more." She reached for her phone and called Mike.

"Mike, what day are we going to Vegas next week?" she asked in a loud, excited voice. "I want to go to Vegas and face that nasty man. I will not let him think he got away with anything," she said in a firm strident voice.

"Well, well," Mike said slowly and softly. "You must have been talking to Joe. Oh, yes, and how are you today, Christine? Are you having a pleasant day?"

"I had a beautiful day until about ten minutes ago," she told him. "I refuse to be Roger's victim. I want to face him while he is in his jail cell and spit in his eye."

"I guess you are a little angry today," Mike said with a grin in his voice.

"I am furious, furious, furious. I took so much crap from that man I…"

Mike interrupted her. "You certainly have earned the right to face him. We need to be there on Tuesday. Our company plane will fly us down and back the same day."

For the next few days, in her mind Christine went through many scenarios of how to act and what to say when she saw Roger. It changed from one minute to the next. Her fury continued to rage. One minute she thought she might be a femme fatale before she lowered the boom on him, and then decided to wear jeans and be very rough with him. Then she decided he wasn't worth that effort. The next morning when Ron stopped to drive her to the airport she was dressed in George's favorite outfit: her black pencil skirt and crisp white shirt and small gold earrings. And of course, her very, very high heeled shoes.

"You look great," Ron told her. "Are you ready to do battle today?"

"Me – do battle?" she asked in a soft whiny voice. "Would I do anything like that?"

Ron started to smile. "I think Roger had better watch out today."

When they met with the federal attorneys in Vegas they learned that the penalty in Nevada for kidnapping is a life sentence. But the case against Roger was not very strong. Roger said it was all Donald's idea. He knew nothing about it. He said Donald was totally responsible for the whole scheme. The D.A. had no eyewitnesses and Roger's fingerprints were not in the area. The fact that a drifter's prints were on the gate of the yard from where Angelo Jo was taken didn't help the case against Roger. And, as for Erin, well, Roger told the police that Erin's parents had pestered him continually, phoning him, begging him for help to get Erin into the music business. The attorneys in Vegas did not feel very comfortable with their case.

The D.A. told Christine that she did not have to agree to meet with Roger, but if she did she should know that Roger's attorney will be with him. She could have her attorney, Mike, with her. Federal officers, Vegas police and others would watch and listen. If she felt uncomfortable at any point she could end the interview. Ron, Mike and Joe would be allowed to watch the conversation.

Christine looked into the room. She saw Roger sitting there wearing a bright orange jump suit. He still had his long stringy hair and long scraggly beard. Roger told authorities he kept his hair long because of his religion. *What religion?* she thought. Christine told Mike she'd go in alone. She stood at the door a minute, then straightened her shoulders and entered the room. She took her time as she made herself comfortable in the chair opposite Roger. She sat quietly staring at Roger.

"Are you really Roger?" she asked.

"It's me, Christine," Roger said sweetly.

"You're not Roger" she said indignantly. "Roger had dark curly hair and a clean, bright smile."

"Christine, it's me."

She paused and glared at him. "Really, is that really you, Roger? Have you been ill? What in the world is wrong?" She paused again. Then with a cold stare in her eyes she looked him in his eyes and said, "Well, what do you want? You asked for this meeting."

Roger turned to his attorney. "I told you she was sassy." Then he turned to Christine. "I keep my hair and beard long for my performances. My fans love my appearance." He gave a sneering smile and continued in a soft mocking voice. "I hope you know that I didn't have any part in this whole episode against you. I would never do that to you Christine. I don't know how Donald got such crazy ideas," he added in a soft condescending voice.

"Really, Roger," she said calmly but kept a bit of a sneer in her voice. "He seemed to know a whole lot about my life back in West Virginia: places I hid as a child when you and I played together, a book I read to my little brother. He called me Tina instead of Christine. No one ever called me that except my folks and brother. If you didn't tell him these things your son must be a mind reader. He seemed to think he knew about the death of my parents and brother. How would he know these things?"

"He must have looked up a lot of old newspapers to get the information. No one knows what happened to your parents. They just disappeared."

"Yeah, sure." Then shaking her head she said, "Roger, Roger. You're still the liar you were when we were married. You need to get with modern technology. I want you to see something." With her right hand opened she laid it on the table. "Do you see these wedding rings? They belonged to my parents."

Christine was wearing the wedding ring of her father on her thumb. On her ring finger she had placed the wedding ring of her mother. "My parents and brother are buried in my mother's family plot in the Blue Ridge Mountains. Roger, I do believe you didn't do enough homework before you thought up this scheme." Christine had great disdain in her voice and mannerisms.

"Well, I don't know how you know that or where you got those rings. No one in town knew anything about your family," he said in a mean voice. Roger began to get very angry and started to rant and rave about various ways he said Christine had abused him and ruined his life. He blamed her for not being the big success he wanted to be. He was very nervous and almost had to be restrained by his attorney. Christine sat there trying to look very bored and disgusted. She signed loudly on occasion. She put her hand up to her face as if she were checking her nail polish as Roger ranted on about various things from her past. Then some of his words finally got to her.

"Say that part again, Roger," she asked.

"I should have known when I said the word 'money' you'd wake up. I said you owe me a million dollars for taking care of you," he shouted at her.

Christine's voice was full of fire. She glared at him but didn't even bat an eyelid as she answered him. "You think I have a million dollars? When I was married to you I lived in the car and took baths in the gas station rest rooms. I washed dishes and bused tables to get food for us to eat. Where do you think I got a million dollars?"

"Your second husband, Leo Martinelli. Everyone knows he was a millionaire. Did you think you could hide that from me? You lived in a penthouse and drove a new Porsche. He left you millions. You and your stupid next husband tried to hide the money by living in an old house, hiding in a little town but I found you. Martinelli made you a millionaire," he snapped back at her.

Christine got very quiet for a minute. Then she spoke, very quietly at first. The intensity of her voice grew as she talked. She leaned over the table and stared into his eyes.

"Leo Martinelli was a member of the mob. He beat me within an inch of my life and killed our baby. Do you want to see the scars that still cover my body? While I was in the hospital fighting for my life the IRS confiscated all of Leo's property to pay his tax bill. He was murdered in jail by another inmate to keep him from telling everything he knew about the mob. I was left with nothing except a hospital bill of half a million dollars. I sold everything I owned, even my clothes to help to pay the bill. I got a job washing dishes in a restaurant." She didn't take her eyes off him as she continued. "Do you remember how I washed dishes to support you? It took me years but I paid off every cent of that hospital bill. If you had done enough research you might have known your plan was very stupid. But it was even more stupid to take a baby away from her family. She may be scarred for life."

Roger sat there and appeared to be shocked as she yelled at him.

Christine continued. "You coerced your young cousin by lying to her and promising her a career. You didn't even have any loyalty to your own family." She paused for a moment. The vision of the guns Donald had carried flashed through her mind. "Tell me Roger, why did Donald carry two guns? Were you that afraid of me?"

"The guns were his idea," Roger told her.

"And I bet you thought it was a great idea. Is that how you planned to kill me?"

Roger's attorney spoke up. "Don't answer that."

"I'll say anything I want," Roger stood up and shouted at his lawyer and then turned to Christine. "I taught my son how to carry a gun and be a man. I wouldn't waste a bullet to finish you off."

The scene was very chaotic. Roger's attorney was yelling, telling Roger to stop talking and tried to push Roger back into his chair. Roger's face got very red and his eyes were wild as he stood there pounding on the table. "We didn't plan to shoot you. We were going to push you off a cliff. Your body would be lost forever."

Christine almost fell off her chair. Her body was shaking and had she tried to stand she might have fallen. But she was determined not to stop her tirade.

"Well, in my opinion there was only one smart thing that might have worked. That was switching the license plates on the cars. Donald was pretty smart to think of that. I guess it made you proud. You weren't bright enough to think of that."

"My son was too dumb to think of it. I was the smart one. I thought of that. I even switched the plates myself."

Roger's attorney stood and insisted the interview was over. He pounded on the window glass to open the door.

But Christine wasn't quite ready to stop talking. She stood, looked at Roger and with the almost sound of a death threat in her voice looked him in the eye and spoke. "Roger, I realized you were a scumbag when I found you in my bed with a young girl. But I'll admit I never thought you'd stoop this low. You are a despicable person to do these things." Christine leaned over the table and spoke very directly to him with her face right in front of his. She continued talking.

"Roger, I am prepared to testify against you with the truth about this whole matter. You are facing a life sentence in prison. I think my testimony will be very powerful. If the DA offers you any sort of deal if you tell everything you know about this plot, I strongly urge you to take it. If by any chance some stupid judge or jury lets you go, I will track you down. I know I will have no trouble finding additional charges. What you did to an innocent family by taking away their baby and the way you treated your own cousin was cruel. If it takes every cent I have, I will follow you and bring you to justice." By this time Christine was almost shouting at him. "Goodbye, Roger. Don't you ever, ever forget this. If you ever are released from jail without serving time I will track you down. I promise you I will be coming after you."

During her tirade, Roger's attorney was shouting that the interview was over. Roger was shouting for her to shut up. The Security Officer had rushed into the room. He quickly removed Christine from the area.

Christine was surrounded by her friends as she left the room. "I feel like I've been through a wringer but it felt good to put that idiot in his place."

"Christine, you were wonderful." "Christine you were very powerful." The praises came both from her friends and members of the local staff who had listened to the conversation. She looked over at her three friends who were standing there with grins on their faces.

Christine, still feeling the emotion of the moment snarled at them saying, "You guys had better wipe those silly grins off your face or I'll start in on you."

"Yes, ma'am, Tiger Lady," they answered.

"Do you need coffee?" Ron finally asked.

"I'll be okay for another five minutes and then I'll probably collapse," she told him. "Do you think he might confess? I do hope that Erin and the baby's parents will not have to go through the ordeal of a trial."

"We'll have to wait and see," Ron told her. Then he turned to Mike and asked if it would be okay to take Christine away from the area for a few minutes. Mike told him that he and Joe were going to be deposed which might take more than an hour. Ron said he'd have her back by then.

As they sat having coffee, a much calmer Christine spoke. "This is the first time I've been back in Vegas since George brought me here to see my daughter's grave many, many years ago. It was the day he told me he loved me and I told him I loved him."

"Try to remember those happy memories instead of the ordeal you have been through today," Ron told her.

"I'm sorry about the way I yelled at you, Mike and Joe. I know I might not be alive today if you had not helped me."

"It's okay, Christine," he said laying his hand over her still shaking hand. "You were absolutely brilliant in there. You should have practiced law."

They sat quietly for a few minutes, neither saying anything.

"Ron, do you think we could possibly grab a cab to visit the cemetery where my baby is buried? George offered to bring me back many times but I was unable to face my past. I think I'm ready now."

"Of course we can," he said. He waved for a passing cab to stop.

"I guess there is nothing about me that you don't know now," she said.

"Christine, I know you are a strong woman. No one gets strong without facing many trials along the way.

Everything I have heard today only increases my respect for you. You really are a special lady."

When they reached the cemetery he asked the cab to wait as Christine went to the grave site. The cemetery was still neatly maintained and was as beautiful as the day she first saw it. She stood there quietly; then with a strong firm walk and a peaceful look on her face, she returned to the cab to go back to the courthouse.

Waiting inside was a couple with a beautiful happy baby girl. "You're Christine and I'm Lisa, Angela Jo's mom. We brought the baby with us so you can see her. How can we ever thank you for taking such good care of her?"

"Oh, she's grown and she's so beautiful," Christine said as she saw the baby.

Angela Jo reached out her little arms for Christine to take her.

"May I hold her," Christine asked.

"Of course."

The baby snuggled down in Christine's arms and began to talk her baby talk to Christine.

"I don't believe she has forgotten you," her father said. "We are so grateful to you for looking after her."

"Well, I never raised a child and wasn't sure exactly what to do, but Erin, even though she is quite young, was very, very good to her."

"Do you think that man will ever confess to the crime?"

"I don't know. I certainly hope so. You must have been frantic with worry and fears when she was missing."

"I pray and hope no other parent ever has to go through such agony. My husband and I are so very, very grateful to you for helping take care of her. There is nothing in the world I can ever do or give you to make up for what you did for me and my family."

"Well, there is one thing you might do," Christine said.

"Whatever might that be?"

"From time to time could you send me her picture? I had a little girl who died right after birth. I was very ill and did not get to hold her. I could only visit her grave. For a little while Angela Jo filled the loneliness I often felt. I'd love get a picture so I can see how she's growing. That would make me feel very happy."

"Of course I'll do that. Please know you are welcome to visit us in our home when you are in the area. I don't believe the baby, deep in her soul, will ever forget you."

Ron, Mike and Joe came into the room to meet the family. The baby was passed to each of them and she had a beautiful smile for them. As the family left the room, Joe said, "I sincerely hope this child will grow up with no recollection of what happed to her."

The Federal Attorney came in and thanked everyone for coming to Vegas. "It appears that Roger has decided to confess about his part in this plot. The staff is talking deal with him. You must have been very persuasive, Mrs. McCall."

"I guess I had a lot of pent-up anger which I vented on him. What sort of deal could he get?"

"About the only thing we can offer is the possibility of parole after twenty years. He would be eighty years old then."

"Well, I'll be eighty years old then, too. That won't be too late for me to track him down and keep my promise."

"Mrs. McCall, I'm glad you are on our side," the attorney said with a smile.

"Maybe you should know a couple things," Christine said quietly. "I did not lie when I was raging against Roger. But I didn't fully explain things either. It wasn't until Ron began to investigate my so-called nephew that I did finally learn how my parents and brother died. A kind lady had retained a box of personal items from the car crash that took their lives. I now have that box. It contained their wedding rings. I didn't plan to use them today. I had them with me as a comfort item. My conversation with Roger didn't go the way I planned. Everything just started to pour out. There is something else you should know. After I healed from the injuries I had sustained from Leo Martinelli, I started a new life. I met George McCall through my employer. We became good friends and fell in love. He was a wonderful man who knew every detail of my life before I met him and he loved me anyway. We had twenty-five wonderful years together. Fortunately for me, he left me enough money so that I could honestly tell Roger I do have enough to track him down. What Roger did to Angela Jo, Erin and me was horrid. Do you feel confident he will go to prison?"

"I don't believe Roger will ever live outside prison," the DA said. "With the official information we have from Mike and Joe, and now from Roger himself, I do not believe we need further depositions from you, Mrs. McCall, nor you, Mr. Davis. You are free to leave whenever you want to go."

Chapter 25

Christine's room seemed very bright with sunshine as she awakened from a restful sleep. She looked at her clock. It was 8:30 a.m. She hadn't slept this late for years. But the bed felt pretty cozy so she nestled back under the covers. She felt good this morning. The Round-The-World Dinner last night had been a huge success. She had a really good time although she didn't sit down much. Small tables for eating had been placed in the center of the hall. Around the perimeter were maps of the world with one or more countries highlighted. In front of the maps were tables representing those countries. At least one table (and sometimes more than one) had food native to that country. Plates were provided for the food as well as mini paper cups for the guest that simply wanted a taste. Another table held objects that pertained to the way of life in that country. The guests browsed through the tables, picked up some food and took it to a smaller table to sit to eat it. Christine's job was to see that no one ran out of food. Teenage youth were the runners from the kitchen. A disc jockey from the local radio station kept a mix of ethnic music playing in the background.

Many people were teasing Joe Sisi because he came wearing his dress uniform.

At one point Ron came to get her telling her he had a surprise. He took her through the crowd to an area by the entrance. There stood Ruth King. With her she had Christine's special friends from the VA Center, Mel, Chuck, Bruce, and Kenny. Beside Kenny, who was in his wheel chair, stood his son and his wife, Ken and Ginny. Christine gave them all a hug. She was very happy to see them.

"Ken and Ginny came by this afternoon to spend time with Kenny. I told them about the big to-do tonight and we decided to have a night out," Ruth said.

"What a wonderful surprise for me," Christine said.

"We read about your ordeal in the paper and were worried about you, but Kenny said it would take more than a nerd to get you down. We're so glad you're okay," Ginny told her.

"I'm just great," Christine said, "but tell me about Ken's surgery. With all the confusion the only news I got from Kenny was that everything went well."

"Ken is doing great," Ginny told her. "Reconciling with his dad made the procedure much easier for him."

As she lay in bed Christine smiled as she remembered the conversation, then her thoughts went back to the dinner. When trying all the various foods had slowed down, Ray asked everyone to be seated. He thanked the guests for coming and told them that another dinner would be held in late winter or early spring. Then he said he had good news.

"I am pleased to announce that we have one door prize to be given tonight. When you came in we asked you to write on your ticket your name and what you think is the biggest asset of our town. We collected the tickets and put them in a fish bowl. Let's ask our mayor to come up and draw the winning door prize. Mayor Wilson, will you please help us?"

The mayor came forward, waved to the crowd and then thanked the committee who had arranged the event. "I am pleased to announce that our door prize will be dinner for four at Eynon's Steak House. May I have the bowl, please?" He started to reach in, then pulled his hand out of the bowl and said. "I think this honor should go to someone else. Someone who loves our city well enough to go the extra mile. May we have a fanfare, please, for one of our finest."

As the fanfare blared, Joe Sisi made his way from the kitchen area wearing his short tunic, gold belt and sandals, and a gold wreath on his head. The crowd roared their approval.

"Joe, will you pull the winning ticket?" the mayor asked him.

Joe pulled the ticket, gave it to the mayor to be read.

"Speech, speech," the crowd cried.

"I love this town," Joe said. He waved to the crowd and returned to the kitchen.

The mayor read the winning entry. It said simply –
The greatest asset? The People.

Christine laid there in bed reliving the night before. *This is a wonderful town* she thought.

She allowed herself another few minutes to relive the evening and then decided she needed to get up. She looked around her bedroom. Never had it been in such a mess. But she had been so busy this summer that everything just got carried there to be put away later.

She saw the relics that had been recovered after Donald had stolen them. She guessed she'd never remember if she got everything back. At least the Civil War items were recovered. The antique shop had wanted a lot of money for them and they had not been sold. Should she just find a permanent home for them in some museum or store them in her attic a while longer, she wondered?

On the floor by her big easy chair were all the newspapers covering the time of Donald/Larry's visit and all the coverage afterward. She hadn't felt like reading them while she was still involved, and there hadn't been time since her trip to Vegas. Maybe she would take time today to read the coverage.

On her dresser she saw the envelope propped against her lamp. It was the letter her mother had written to her that she never received. The letter that was in the box sent from Virginia. Though she had carefully read every newspaper and official reports that were in the box as well as going through all the treasures, Christine was having a hard time opening this letter from her mother. *Maybe I'll do it later today* she thought. She went to the kitchen to get her coffee.

Her phone began to ring nonstop as she and her friends relived every minute of the night before. The morning and afternoon passed quickly.

Her phone rang again in the late afternoon. "Want to grab a light supper down at the diner?" Ron asked her.

"I'd like that," she told him, "but I need some time to get cleaned up. I've been on the phone all day."

As she returned home she thought about what an easy relationship she had entered into with Ron. She felt like she really had a best friend, one with who she could always be herself. He certainly knew every part of her past life. He had lost the love of his life just as she had. Yet he had made a new life and had moved on. His daughter and family who lived in the area had invited her to share a Sunday dinner and a late summer picnic. Mike and his family had also invited her to share several outings with them. In many ways Christine felt as if she had a great big family.

But as she saw the envelope written by her mother on her dresser that night, she felt the time had come for her to read the last message her mother had tried to send her. She held the envelope in her hands, really looking at the hand writing of her mother with both the return address of home and the address where Christine had once lived with Roger. She saw the special stamp on the front, "Return to Sender – Occupant Moved – No Forwarding Address."

She carefully opened the envelope and started to read.

September 10th

My darling daughter,

I'm writing to you tonight to share with you some exciting news which is making your dad, your brother and I very happy. I hope it makes you happy as well. At the end of the month, we will be leaving West Virginia and moving to Nashville.

The man who owned the bar your father managed for so many years decided to sell it. The new owner plans to move into the apartment upstairs that was our home for so many years. Your dad's former boss did offer your dad the opportunity to manage a bar in a little town not too far from Nashville.

As I'm sure you'll remember, your dad only took this job while he was recovering from the mine accident. But somehow it lasted all these years. Now we have an opportunity to try to find the life we have dreamed about.

I can't begin to tell you how much we have missed you. We have felt so much sorrow over not having you with us. Dad has always regretted that he pushed you into such a quick marriage. I regret that I wasn't strong enough to stand up to him. But we both hope you and Roger have found happiness together, and that you are well and happy.

Each year since we have been married we have saved $1,000. It has now become our nest egg to help us relocate. We plan to buy a small house hopefully not too far for us to see you often. We don't want to run your life, just be able to see you again. You will never know how much we have missed you. Little Larry is dancing on air because he wants to see his Tina.

The official date for us to leave here is September 30th. We have already transferred our funds to the First National Bank of Nashville so you know we are very serious about this move. Dad said that as a special treat for me that we will travel down to my childhood home in Virginia. I hope I can find some relatives still living there.

We love you and miss you so much. We can't wait to see you. Give our love to Roger but keep tons of it for yourself.

Love,
Mom

Christine held the letter in her hands, carefully running her fingers over the written words. *They weren't mad at me. They did love me. They tried to let me know where they would be so I could find them.* She let the tears fall silently down her cheeks, read the letter two more times, and then put it under her pillow and tried to sleep.

Chapter 26

In a rather somber mood the next morning, she carried all the newspapers she had accumulated downstairs. She had been somewhat reluctant to read them, but decided they were ghosts in the room. She wanted them gone. She fixed some coffee and began to read the papers. The first day the stories had focused on the arrest of a man trying to pull a scam on a local resident. He claimed he was a relative. By the second day the kidnapping was the main story. As the reports unfolded, they did seem to be pretty factual. They mentioned Christine McCall, widow of the late George McCall, etc. The stories did delve into Christine's past. But the reports were not unkind. They dwelt on the marriage of two seventeen year-olds which ended in divorce. There was a brief report about a second marriage to Leo Martinelli which ended with the death of both Mr. Martinelli and their infant daughter. Only one out-of-town newspaper told of Christine's days as a bar maid and her days with Leo and the terrible beating he had given her. There were big reports on her marriage to George McCall, Crofton's own hometown son. Some of the other papers had a few more details. The reports did not make Christine a guardian angel that saved a baby and teen-age girl, but neither did they seem to print all the mistakes of her early life.

Christine sat at her table and thought of how afraid she had been all these years. Afraid that someone would tell about her past. Afraid that someone would make her the talk of the town because of her past. Somehow she had always thought that people were nice to her because of their respect for George. When he died she didn't have the security of knowing he was there to help her through any gossip or feelings of hurt and anger. She slowly came to realize that it didn't really matter to her if everyone knew about her past. Yes, she made some dumb mistakes, but many people have also done so. She picked up all the papers and put them into the recycling bin. *My past is really past now,* she thought.

She decided this was a good day to get back to her old routine. She tried a new recipe for a chicken and rice dish which she put into the individual casseroles for Henry and Ed. She mixed up a refrigerator roll recipe that let her pull off just as much dough as she needed for that day to have ready to go with the chicken. Then she remembered how much those two men loved her cookies. She reached for her flour bin and began to make some Chocolate Chip Cookies and some Snickerdoodles. Ed and Henry really loved them.

Christine cleaned up her kitchen, packed up the food she had prepared and headed for the Retirement Village. Henry was very happy to see her and invited her in for coffee. Ed was there visiting him so the three sat to visit while they drank their coffee and ate cookies.

"Christine, you've been through a pretty bad time this summer. Are you doing okay?" Henry asked her.

"Did you shudder when you read about all the bad things I've done in my life?" she asked the men. "Were you disappointed that George chose someone with my past to spend his life with?" she asked them.

"George told us he had met the most wonderful woman in the world right after he met you. We were happy for him."

They sat and reminisced about George for a while and then she left for home. While she was driving home her cell phone rang. She saw from the I.D. it was Mike calling. Since she was stopped at a red light she answered her phone.

"I have something for you, Christine," he said. "Will it be okay if Pat and I stop by tonight?"

"Of course, but what's going on? No new problems, I hope."

"Not at all. Just a few loose ends to tie up. See you about seven-thirty."

Prior to the *episode* as she called it, Mike had never been in her home. Now he wants to stop by. *This is very nice* she thought.

"I brought my wife with me because I might be doing something I shouldn't do," he told her when they arrived.

"You have me really puzzled," she told him. "What's going on?"

"I received a package a few days ago. Apparently the sender got my name from the newspapers. There are two letters you need to read before you look at the package. There was a book written about you many years ago. Only one copy was printed. Everything is explained in the letters. I want to be honest with you. I nearly pitched the whole thing, but I was curious so I took it home and read it. It is extremely well-written and appears to be a very honest book. I had planned to toss the whole thing if I found it hurtful to you in any way."

"Please don't be mad at me, Christine," Pat said, "but when I saw him so engrossed in it I also read it. I promise you I will never tell a single person about it if that's what you wish, but it is a moving, loving story."

"I don't understand," Christine said. "A book about me. What in the world…?"

"The two letters will explain everything. We must leave now; we're going to be late for our dance lessons. Can you believe I'm learning how to do the cha-cha?"

"Sound like fun. I'll look at this and call you tomorrow."

Christine looked at the two letters. They were written by two different people with the same last name. Mike had posted a yellow sticky note on one that said, *Read First.*

Feeling very puzzled, she began to read.

To: Michael Rosen, Attorney for Christine McCall

Forty years ago my father was a cub reporter just starting his career. He was in a bar in Vegas one night relaxing when he noticed his favorite waitress, a young woman with porcelain skin and red hair and a very shapely body had for some reason dyed her beautiful hair coal black. All the other wait staff, as well as some of regular customers were teasing her. Apparently she fell for some line about getting in the movies.

My father was an ambitious young man who thought it would make a very good human interest story so began to try to learn more about her. For the next few years he investigated all about her when he was not on assignment. He began to think it might make a very interesting book. When he was sent overseas our family thought the quest for his story was over, but a couple of years later when he came home he again began to search for her. But one day he said the search was over. He never fully explained why he changed his mind. He had one copy of his book printed and put away in his many files.

You may or may not recognize his name. My father was a world famous war journalist who won many awards. He died in the spring of this year. In going through his papers, we found the book and the accompanying letter. It is self-explanatory. My family and I made a decision to send the book to Christine McCall. Please see that she gets this copy. She can read it and throw it away. Or she can have it published. We want no money from this book. We do hope

that if she does decide to publish it she will give
due credit to my father. He was a good honest
and honorable man.

> *Sincerely,*
> *Grant Ross*

Very puzzled Christine reached for the second letter.
She saw it was written by the man who had written the
book, J. W. Ross.

To *Whom It May Concern:*

> *Many years ago when I was starting my career*
> *I met a young waitress in a bar in Las Vegas.*
> *I became fascinated with her bright red hair, a*
> *shapely body, and beautiful skin you felt you could*
> *see through. No, I did not fall in love with her. I*
> *was already married to the love of my life, but I*
> *was unable to get this woman out of my mind.*
> *I wrote story after story about her: why she was*
> *working in a bar, where she was from, etc. One*
> *day I realized that I was creating a book so decided*
> *to get facts instead of fantasy. In talking with other*
> *people I learned her name was Christine and she*
> *was from West Virginia. On a trip east on business*
> *I traveled to her home town. I traveled a lot for my*
> *job and lost track of her for a year or so. But I was*
> *able to track her move back to Las Vegas.*
> *When the story made the news in the Leo*
> *Martinelli case, I realized that his wife was*

Christine Stewart Parker. I'm ashamed to say I became a stalker. I hounded the hospital staff and even tried to bribe them to get information on Christine. I learned about the birth and death of her daughter. It wasn't too difficult to learn where the baby was buried. Shortly after, I was sent overseas on another assignment. When I came back after a couple of years, Christine's story continued to haunt me. I learned she had left town. About once or twice a year I remembered about the grave site of her daughter and visited it. A few years later I went once more to visit the site. When I was leaving the area I saw Christine get out of a car. She was even more beautiful and fascinating than I remembered. She was carrying a bouquet which she placed on the grave. She was with a man whom I knew from his demeanor cared deeply for her. I felt as if I was glued to the spot. I watched as the man consoled her. And then I watched the miracle of seeing two people either fall in love, or at least admit their feelings of love for each other. I stood for a long time watching them. I didn't need to hear the words to know what was happening. I saw them cry and get angry about something. They appeared to be working through something of great sorrow. Finally, I saw them stand and embrace each other. I felt their love for each other even as I stood across the street and tried to hide behind bushes. I traced the man by using the car license. I learned it was a car rented by George McCall of Crofton, California, a man well-known in the investment business. I kept track of them for almost a year.

I realized I had my story. But I also realized that this should never be published or sold. It was too personal, too deep.

One day I decided to have one copy printed only to show I did have a softer side to my writing than all the tragedies of war I have written about.

To my precious wife I want to say thank you for letting me have this long distance love affair with another woman I never met and who didn't even know I existed.

I hope you always knew you were first in my life. You made me the man I am today.

> *Love,*
> *J.W.*

Christine reached into the mailer envelope and removed the nicely bound copy of the book. It was titled simply

Christine
A Story of Courage

Christine didn't quite know what to think. She wasn't sure she wanted to know what was written about her. On one hand she felt a little violated that someone had stalked her, but a part of her was curious about what was written. She lived the part. Did she really want to re-live everything again? *Probably not much of it is true anyhow,* she thought. She laid it aside and went to bed. But after tossing and turning a lot, she got up, fixed some tea and sat down to read the book. She soon lost herself in the well-written story and saw *Christine* as a character in the story, not as the person who lived it. She laughed at parts, especially the part about her black hair, and cried at the end. *Oh, George,* she thought. *I wish you were here to share this story with me.* She laid it aside and had a pleasant night of sleep.

Chapter 27

Christine made a slow walk through her house, from the attic to the basement. She wanted to be sure things were put away and no empty coffee cups were setting around before she headed for France. She had packed her big suitcase this morning and had only a few things left to put in her carry-on bag. Her refrigerator was nearly empty and all the trash had been stowed in the bins for pick-up. Elaine told her Roy would put the bins out on pick-up day. She had made arrangements for Elaine and Roy to stop by and see her friends at the VA while she was gone. Christine didn't want them to be forgotten. Betty and Ray said they planned to keep in touch with Ed and Henry. There were still a few legal things coming up about Roger and Donald but nothing she needed to be here for.

She had a nice note from Angela Jo's mother with two pictures: one of baby Angela Jo and one of the three children together. She said the baby was doing well. Christine smiled as she thought about Erin. Erin's letters had gone from letters about her embarrassment to return to her friends and school, to nice letters about her life, her boy friend, her term paper for science which was going to be on otters, and the fact that she was a soloist in the school choir. Ruth King had told her that her daughter's plans for the troubled teenagers was moving full steam ahead and she planned to have her first class of training at the first of the year. *Life is good* Christine thought.

Satisfied that she had everything in good order, she grabbed her windbreaker and back pack from the hook in the walk-in pantry and headed for her car. This was her first visit to the rock on the shoreline since spring. Christine hardly believed it had been so long. *I guess I had no one else to really talk with before this summer. Now I am surrounded by friends who keep me busy,* she thought. As she drove along she thought about the last time she had made this trip. It was the trip she made with so-called Larry, Jody and baby Bella. *What a change that episode made in my life.* Then she started to smile. *If only George could see me now,* she laughed. She seemed to live in jeans and sweatshirts. Her high-heels were saved for special occasions. She wondered if she should dress up more when she got to France. Somehow she thought she'd be in jeans.

After much soul-searching she had decided to go to see Bob and Mimi. But she decided not to stay all winter. She'd come home right after Christmas. There were people here who needed her. Bob and Mimi's daughter, Jeannine, who was George's godchild and almost as old as Christine, planned to meet her at a hotel in Paris. After a few days of shopping and letting Christine rest up a bit, they planned to drive south to the family home. She began to get excited about getting to see these dear people.

When Christine arrived at the parking lot at the start of the trail along the coastline, she saw the concession stand had been closed for the winter. It was nearly the end of October; the trees were turning color and the bright sun was making sparkling diamonds on the calm ocean water. She hoisted her backpack on her shoulder and began her walk along the trail. She stopped to visit the family of otters and remembered how much Erin had loved them. When she reached the rock, she opened her pack and took out a bright red crispy apple. She took a bite and sat there quietly for a few minutes. Then she began to talk to George.

"I want you to know what has been going on in my life so you aren't mad at me for not coming here to talk to you for such a long time. I had quite a summer; most of it wasn't too bad because I knew you were watching out for me. I still kissed your picture every night. I'll try to forget all the bad things that happened and remember all the good things: the new friends I made, the people I helped and mostly the people who helped me.

"The most important thing was that I learned about my family. Even though I did realize they were probably dead, it has helped me to know it for sure. And to know they are buried in the cemetery with other family members helped me to feel a sense of closure about it.

"Another important thing that happened is that I have started to spend your money. George, George, I hope your efforts to leave money for me to live on after you were gone never kept you from having everything you wanted. It wasn't until Mike really forced me to look at the numbers that I realized what a fortune you left behind for me. Mike has encouraged me to spend it. I doubt I'll ever spend it all but I have had a great pleasure in how I have spent it so far. I arranged for a memory garden to be established at the VA Center. I think those men and women there will enjoy a *walk in the park* or even take a book to read while sitting in a quiet grove of trees. I asked Ron to manage the work but he still feels it necessary to get my approval. I think there will be a wonderful sense of calm and peace there which is missing from the inside of the buildings.

"I also gave Joe Sisi some money to start his youth center. He got space in what was the car dealership down on Market Street. His plans call for a big gym (for basketball), another room with pool and ping pong tables, as well as tables just to sit and talk. At the end of the building are smaller rooms. He is recruiting business people in town to come and help tutor the students with everything from better reading skills to math and science help. The response from the town has been overwhelming.

"I also endowed some money for Mike to use however he sees fit at the university. I don't know what he'll finally decide, but I know he is thinking very seriously about scholarships.

"I had a wonderful time helping with a big community event we called The Round the World Dinner. I worked with both men and women in the town and found them all to be friendly and pleasant. It makes me wonder about something. Did the people really tend to see me as a femme fatale or did I imagine it? I think I did worry about that more than I should have. I feel I have now closed the door on that part of my life. Even though all the dark secrets of my past have been exposed, I have more friends now than I ever had in my life.

"I really treasure the box I received from Virginia which had the items from the car and reports of the accident which took the life of my family. The most precious thing was the letter from my mother. I am so sorry my parents didn't get to meet and know you. They would have loved you like I did. My mother told me in the letter they had money saved and transferred to a bank in Nashville to prepare for their move there. I asked Mike to trace the money. He was able to recover between $10-$15 thousand dollars. I have decided I will add to the amount and give it to the little town that buried my family. I do so want to thank them for the love and honor they bestowed on people they didn't even know. I'm going to do it in person.

"Early tomorrow morning, Ron and I will be on Mike's company plane. Mike has arranged for it to stop at a small airport in western Virginia on a trip the plane is making to Washington, D.C. Ron has arranged for his friend Deke to meet us there. We will go to the cemetery to visit the gravesites of my parents.

"We will then have lunch with the nice lady who saved the treasures for me and I will give her a check. Ron told Deke about the check and he feels that Deke will have told someone who told someone else and that the mayor and newspaper may be involved. We'll see.

"Then we will drive to Washington, D.C. where Ron will drop me off at the airport hotel. He will drive on to visit his son who is in D.C. I have a seven a.m. departure time the next morning to go to see Bob and Mimi. I need to check in around 5 a.m. Your godchild, Jeanine, has called me repeatedly saying her folks are anxious to see if I'm really okay. I'm sure that being with them will once again make me feel so close to you. I plan to go to our favorite spot where we sat and watched all the cruise ships and played various games about who was on them. Remember the time we were watching the ship that we pretended had the king and queen of England on it? Remember our surprise when we found out we really did see that ship.

"There is something amazing that has happened. I know that the special day we declared our love for each other was one when we thought we were the only people on the earth. Well, it turns out we were being watched. Watched by a reporter, one of the ones who had followed me for years. But it turns out he was not a scumbag. He said he felt he was watching something special that day. As he watched us declare our love for each other he decided it really was a special kind of love and one that should be kept private. He had followed me for many years. He did write his book and had one copy printed which his family sent to me. I read it twice, once reading it knowing it was about me. Then I read it again and let the character speak to me. He had done a lot of research on my life and had things in it I had forgotten about. I believe he must have talked with someone in Roger's family because he knew a lot about my early life and my life with Roger. The story followed my life to Vegas and had many details about my life there as well as the horrible details of my marriage to Leo. The story ended with our marriage. He made me look like someone really special and he certainly got you right: a very, very good man with a heart of gold.

"You know something, George? As excited as I am about going to Europe, I am also excited about coming home. Crofton is a wonderful place to live. The people are wonderful. I will be coming home to many friends who have already planned many projects for me.

"Thank you, George, for everything, for choosing me to marry, for bringing me to this town, for taking care of me for so many years and showing me the world. You took good care of me, not only with money, but with good friends and good people."

Christine sat there quietly for a few minutes, just resting and letting her mind wander over many things. Then she stood, picked up her backpack, blew a kiss to the ocean and made her way back to her car and to the rest of the world.

"See you later, George."